Readers love *Rekindled Flame* by ANDREW GREY

"Definitely a well done and uplifting story."
—My Fiction Nook

"What a fantastic, multilayered, and emotionally moving book!"
—Rainbow Book Reviews

"*Rekindled Flame* is another well written story from Andrew Grey. There's danger and suspense and, as always, there's that great feeling of camaraderie, support and a sweet HEA."
—The Novel Approach

"This was a beautiful and at times suspenseful tale."
—Diverse Reader

D1563094

More praise for
ANDREW GREY

Eyes Only for You

"Andrew Grey is truly a spectacular author and writes books that make an impact on the readers."

—Gay Book Reviews

"It was hot and frustrating and sweet. Also quite romantic. Many things that make an Andrew Grey book great!"

—Diverse Reader

The Playmaker

"This is a story for people looking for a nice getaway. It's light, low on angst, has a few hot smexy times, and is lovely in the way that Andrew Grey books always are."

—Open Skky Book Reviews

"Another must read from Andrew Grey."

—Scattered Thoughts and Rogue Words

Noble Intentions

"This is a really sweet story. I loved the pacing and the careful revelation of character and motivation."

—Joyfully Jay

"This is a good read for anyone who likes Andrew Grey (come back for this one), and enjoys a quick read with some nobility thrown in. English accents, internet wizards and down-to-earth men – definitely worth picking up."

—Alpha Book Club

By Andrew Grey

Accompanied by a Waltz
Between Loathing and Love
Can't Live Without You
Chasing the Dream
Crossing Divides
Dominant Chord
Dutch Treat
Eastern Cowboy
In Search of a Story
Noble Intentions
North to the Future
One Good Deed
Path Not Taken
Planting His Dream
The Playmaker
Saving Faithless Creek
Shared Revelations
Stranded • Taken
Three Fates
(Multiple Author Anthology)
To Have, Hold, and Let Go
Turning the Page
Whipped Cream

HOLIDAY STORIES
Copping a Sweetest Day Feel
Cruise for Christmas
A Lion in Tails
Mariah the Christmas Moose
A Present in Swaddling Clothes
Simple Gifts • Snowbound in
Nowhere • Stardust

ART
Legal Artistry • Artistic Appeal
Artistic Pursuits • Legal Tender

BOTTLED UP
The Best Revenge • Bottled Up
Uncorked
An Unexpected Vintage

BRONCO'S BOYS
Inside Out • Upside Down
Backward • Round and Round

THE BULLRIDERS
A Wild Ride • A Daring Ride
A Courageous Ride

BY FIRE
Redemption by Fire
Strengthened by Fire
Burnished by Fire
Heat Under Fire

CARLISLE COPS
Fire and Water • Fire and Ice
Fire and Rain
Fire and Snow • Fire and Hail

CHEMISTRY
Organic Chemistry
Biochemistry • Electrochemistry

DREAMSPUN DESIRES
#4 – The Lone Rancher
#28 – Poppy's Secre

EYES OF LOVE
Eyes Only for Me
Eyes Only for You

Published by Dreamspinner Press
www.dreamspinnerpress.com

By ANDREW GREY (CONT.)

Published by DREAMSPINNER PRESS
www.dreamspinnerpress.com

CLEANSING FLAME
ANDREW GREY

Published by

DREAMSPINNER PRESS

5032 Capital Circle SW, Suite 2, PMB# 279, Tallahassee, FL 32305-7886 USA
www.dreamspinnerpress.com

Cleansing Flame
© 2017 Andrew Grey.

Cover Art
© 2017 L.C. Chase.
http://www.lcchase.com
Cover content is for illustrative purposes only and any person depicted on the cover is a model.

ISBN: 978-1-63533-487-6
Digital ISBN: 978-1-63533-488-3
Library of Congress Control Number: 2017901539
Published March 2017
v. 1.0

Printed in the United States of America
♾
This paper meets the requirements of
ANSI/NISO Z39.48-1992 (Permanence of Paper).

For Dominic.
He isn't a firefighter, but as both of us get on into middle age,
he still lights a fire for me.

Chapter 1

SOMETIMES IT really sucked being older than everybody else, and sometimes it was an advantage. For the last four years, Dayne Mills had gone to school in order to graduate from college, and closing in on thirty, he was finally near the finish line. He had chosen a degree in the humanities, with the goal of being able to teach. At least that was the plan. Get an education so he could get a job and better support himself and hopefully leave some of his past behind. He had begun to second-guess that plan about a year ago, but it had been too late to change course.

Dayne's faculty advisor had pulled a lot of strings for him, so instead of sitting in his usual building at Penn State Harrisburg, he was in Carlisle at Dickinson College, taking two classes he could never have afforded otherwise. Professor Collins was an amazing man who thought Dayne had talent, so he'd arranged for him to take more advanced classes at Dickinson for a semester. It was unusual, and Dayne was honored that Professor Collins and the people at Dickinson had been willing to work to make this happen.

Instead of meeting in a fancy lecture hall, their class was in one of the older buildings on campus, in a room with tables formed into a square so everyone could see one another. Dayne had been a little awed when he'd first walked in a month ago. This wasn't like the modern white-walled classroom he was used to, with plain desks and A/V equipment. This room had towering ceilings and windows that reached all the way to them, surrounded by warm woodwork that had been there for over a century. Every time he came to class at Dickinson, he wished more than anything that he'd gone here for all of his education.

"Good morning." Professor Hunterson strode into class and set his books on the table.

"Good morning," Dayne muttered half under his breath. While the other students were chipper and excited, he was tired. He'd been up most of the night because his legs refused to stop throbbing. They still ached, but concentrating on the discussion took his mind off them.

"As all of you know from the syllabus, part of this class is a paper on some facet of the history of American education. I'd like to review the topics you've chosen. I've already talked with some of you, but for those I haven't, please see me during the last fifteen minutes of class."

Dayne opened his notebook and looked at the ideas he'd jotted down for his paper, the general topics ranging from the birth of public education to education on the American frontier. He really didn't think too much of any of them. They sounded so predictable and ordinary, and he wanted to do something special and interesting. He stared at the page for a few more seconds, hoping inspiration would strike, but nothing came to him. Not that he had much time—the discussion was starting.

"Let's start where we left off talking about the national education policy during World War II." Professor Hunterson did a quick review of the details he wanted to focus on from the reading material and then opened the class to discussion.

Dayne both loved and hated this style. He loved it because it was so different from the conventional lecture-type classes he got at Penn State Harrisburg. These classes were exciting, with students arguing with one another and sometimes even with the professor in order to fully flesh out concepts and ideas. He also hated it for the same reason. Talking in front of others always made his stomach churn. Dayne knew Professor Hunterson kept track of everyone who spoke, so he got his thoughts together and shared them with the class. "The austerity during the war definitely extended to the classrooms."

"Yes. That's a topic I've been waiting for," Professor Hunterson said after Dayne croaked out his thoughts. The class picked up on the theme, and before long Dayne was in a lively discussion and hardly had time to think much about it.

"That's all we have time for today," Professor Hunterson said a while later, "but we'll pick this up next time." Most of the students grabbed their notebooks and filed out, but Dayne stayed behind, once again looking at his ideas. Three other students did also, and Dayne remained seated while each of them talked to the professor for a few minutes and then departed.

Dayne shifted and pushed on the table to help himself stand, but Professor Hunterson got up, walked to where he was, and sat next to him.

"You're doing very well in class. I know participating is hard for you."

"Yes, it can be sometimes."

"But you have some great ideas. Continue to share them." He smiled, and Dayne's nerves dissipated. He liked the professor. Dayne guessed he was in his early fifties. He had thinning gray hair and eyes that always seemed just on the edge of joy. He was clearly a happy man, something Dayne was jealous of.

"I will. Thank you." He relaxed and opened his notes to the ideas he had for his paper. "I came up with all these, but none of them are good enough." Dayne hated showing Professor Hunterson the paper and was shocked when the professor chuckled. "See, I knew they were bad."

"No. I could use this list as an assignment sheet for the papers the next time I teach this class. You don't have bad ideas. These are all really good and doable in the time frame you have. I'd say your problem is deciding which of these you're most excited about."

Dayne gawked at him and then turned away, embarrassed, his hand shaking as he tried to decide if he was being joked with. Apparently he wasn't, judging by Professor Hunterson's warm smile. "Oh."

"Definitely. Personally I like this one." He pointed to *Carlisle Indian School*. Dayne had just been jotting down a list of ideas freeform, and that had come up. He wasn't even sure where he'd heard of it, other than knowing Jim Thorpe had gone there and seeing references to it in the library. "Think of it as a study in good intentions."

Dayne smiled and nodded. "I liked that one too, only because it would give me something new to dig into."

"But you need to find an angle in order to make your paper interesting. We can write all the bare facts we want about the number of students who went there or the classes offered, as well as how long the school operated—and those *should* be in the paper—but it's the human story about the students that will make it worth reading."

"Okay. I think I'd like that."

Professor Hunterson glanced at the clock on the wall and then stood. "I'm about to lose this room to another class. Do you need to get somewhere else? I don't want to keep you."

"No. This is my last class of the day, and I was going to head over to the library to try to get started." Now that he'd picked his topic, he was excited and raring to go.

"You could, but in addition to the materials the college has, there are also extensive materials at the historical society. If you want my opinion, I'd start there." He gathered his stuff and left the room.

Dayne groaned, got to his feet, and walked slowly to work the stiffness out of his legs. Thankfully the historical society was just a few blocks away, so he wasn't going to have to walk very far.

"HOW CAN I help you?" the retirement-aged lady in a bright patterned blouse asked as Dayne approached the desk.

"Yes. I understand you have materials from the Carlisle Indian Industrial School?"

"Yes, we do. If you'd please sign in for me, I can get someone to help you." She indicated the mounted tablet, and Dayne filled out the information requested. She talked on the phone briefly and then hung up. "Beverly is in the library, down the hall to your left, and she can assist you."

"Thank you." He walked slowly and tried not to wince. He should have brought his cane from the car today, but he hated the damned thing. It made him feel like an old man when he was only twenty-six, for fuck's sake. Dayne gritted his teeth and stopped, waiting for the tinge of pain to drain away. Then he carried on.

To his right was a museum of sorts, with displays that visitors could wander through. He would have liked to do that, but today wasn't the day for extra walking. He continued down the bright, newly painted hallway and turned into a large room with tables set in the center and a few desks around the side. Framed maps and drawings of the town and surrounding area hung on the walls. Dayne sat at the nearest chair he could find, pulled out the chair next to it, and propped his left leg up on it to rub his upper thigh. He closed his eyes as the muscles slowly began to relax.

"May I help you?" the woman asked curtly from the desk. The tiredness in her eyes reminded him of his mother toward the end of her life, and Dayne had to mentally boost himself to keep out of that sad place. He had work to do.

"I think so. If you could give me a minute, I'll be over." The desk wasn't far, but at that moment, the damn thing might as well have been positioned on top of Everest. To his relief, she stood and walked to where he sat, using her cane as she moved. "I'm sorry." Dayne felt badly as she took the seat across from him.

"I know a hard day for someone when I see it. I've had my fair share of them." She looked up and motioned to one of the other women, who hurried over. "Joanie, there's a pot of tea in the back. Would you please pour two cups and bring them out for us?" Joanie nodded and hurried away. "I know a man in need of a drink when I see one, though tea is all I can offer here. If I were home, I'd put a dab of whiskey in it."

Dayne grinned. "I know the feeling well."

"So, what can I do for you, young man?"

"I'm taking a class at Dickinson, and I'm writing a paper on the Carlisle Indian Industrial School, but I don't want to do the usual blah, blah thing. I know Dickinson has materials, but I was hoping

5

you might have some information on the students. What was life like for them? Did they enjoy being at the school? Was it a happy place for them or one of hardship? How did going there affect their lives, good or bad?"

"That's quite a bit. We have some of the school records…." Beverly thought. "We also have student material—reports and things like that. There are some pictures as well. But…." She smiled. "What I think you'll want to see most are the journals. We have some student journals that were kept while they were at the school."

Joanie returned with two Styrofoam cups with lids, and she set one in front of each of them.

"Thank you," Dayne said. He wasn't much of a tea drinker, but he wasn't going to spurn Beverly's kindness. He sipped from the cup. "Wow." It was smooth, gentle, and warmed him from the inside out. Just what he needed after his walk in the early fall chill.

"Glad you like it." Beverly turned to Joanie and asked her to get the journals Dayne needed. "Third row on your right, three tracks down, second shelf from the top."

Joanie ran off to do Beverly's bidding.

"I appreciate your help." Dayne took another sip of tea as a man strode into the room and looked around. He was tall and broad, with intense dark eyes and a determined set to his lips.

"I will be with you in just a minute," Beverly told him.

Dayne lifted his cup to his lips once again, watching the man and trying not to look like he was doing so. He was gorgeous, and while Dayne knew a guy like that would never look at him twice, he figured there was no harm in a little wishing. Okay, from the way those black jeans hugged his thighs and his T-shirt stretched over his arms and chest, maybe a lot of wishing, because… wow, just wow.

Joanie returned and placed two bound books on the table, along with what looked like some old composition books.

"That's them. Thank you."

"Yes. I appreciate all your help." Dayne smiled, and Joanie hurried back to what she'd been doing.

"Thank you so much for the help and the tea," he said, knowing Beverly had other things to do.

She stood, picking up her tea, and took it back to her desk, where she talked with the man, who now had his back to Dayne. He got the full-on view of a backside worthy of being carved into marble, and of wide shoulders, narrow hips. Dayne was glad he was seated at a table because he popped wood right there just looking at the guy. Of course, his leg picked that moment to throb, and that was always a buzzkill.

"I'm sorry, but I'm sure we don't have what you're looking for. I can check, though." Beverly got up and used her cane to walk to the other room, where Dayne could see the rows of shelves through the open door.

The man turned around, and Dayne looked away, not wanting to get caught staring, even though it was hard as hell. Come to think of it, so was Dayne.

He reached for the nearest book, opened it, and tried like the devil to read the handwriting on the page.

"Excuse me."

Dayne looked up from his book and into the darkest eyes he had ever seen. A shiver raced up his back, and he knew his mouth hung open like he was doing a fish imitation. "Yes?"

"Is it okay if I sit down?"

"Sure." Dayne did his best not to act dumb or anything.

Tall, Dark, and Handsome pulled out the chair and sat with his legs spread, one bouncing up and down nervously. "What kind of research are you doing?" he asked, and Dayne realized he was going to have to say more than a few words to this guy.

"Just some things for class." He waved, indicating the journals on the table.

"That's cool. Do you go to Dickinson?" He flashed a smile.

Dayne smiled in return. "It's complicated, but yes." He lowered his gaze and returned to the diary in front of him. The first entry was from January 1, 1901, by a student named Yellow Bird, though once he was at school, he was called Berty. Dayne tried to read, but his attention was on the man watching him from across the table. "Is something wrong?"

The man winked, and Dayne blushed big-time. He lowered his gaze once again and read about how cold it was and what Berty had for dinner after settling in his room. It was ordinary and kind of boring. Dayne skimmed the next entry and the following ones.

"I'm sorry, but I don't have what you're looking for," Beverly said once she returned from the stacks.

The smile slipped from the man's face, and he stood. "Thank you for looking." He turned and left the room.

Dayne followed him with his gaze, unable to stop himself, and then returned to his reading.

Over the next hour, he read through two of the journals. He did get some information, especially on how some of the boys felt about being sent across the country, away from their families. He made copies of those references, thinking he might be able to use them, and continued on. It didn't take very long to review the last journals and to make copies of the important pages he might need. There wasn't enough to build a paper on, but some ideas were starting to form.

"Beverly, are these all of them?" he asked.

"Yes. There are some letters as well."

As she got up, Dayne saw a familiar pain in her eyes. He looked for Joanie, but she wasn't around. "Just tell me where they are and I promise not to touch anything else." He went over to her and stood at the door. "I know what it's like to feel like your legs have betrayed you."

"Third row on your right, fourth rack, and they're on either the third or fourth shelf. They're in a loose-leaf folder. Look at the tabs and you'll find them."

Dayne thanked her and entered the room. It was large, with movable racks that cranked to expose the desired portion. Thankfully the one he needed was already open from before, and he hobbled down to the section Beverly had indicated. Everything was catalogued beautifully, and he easily found the letters he was looking for, along with some other things that piqued his interest. He knew he'd be spending a lot more time here.

He retrieved the letters, returned, and showed them to Beverly so she could make a notation of what he had. "Can I ask about the boxes on the bottom of the racks?"

"They're one of our future projects. We received a donation of materials a few months ago, and when I saw they pertained to the school, I put them there until I had time to catalog them." She shook her head. "There's never enough time to get everything done."

Dayne nodded and took the letters to his table. He started reading, and after a few minutes, Beverly set some additional materials beside him, including what looked like another journal. After some time had gone by, Joanie added one of the boxes he'd seen in the back.

Beverly shifted to the table and began going through it carefully. "There are two other boxes besides this. I'll get them catalogued, and if I find anything of promise, I'll save it for you." She turned to the clock, and Dayne followed her gaze. The society was closing in half an hour, and Dayne had to get home soon.

"Thank you. I have class again on Wednesday, but I was hoping to continue working tomorrow."

"Then maybe you can help me." She smiled, and Dayne nodded.

"Can I take this journal with me? I know it's not catalogued yet, but it would really help."

"I think that would be okay. Sign it out before you go, okay?" She got up and moved toward her desk.

He finished reviewing the letters and placed them on Beverly's desk before thanking her for all her help, signing the journal out, and slowly leaving the building. The pain in his legs had dissipated, and the walk to his car loosened the muscles enough that he was moving pretty well. Things were looking up. He had an idea for his paper, and he'd gotten some of the research done. Well, at least he'd made progress on finding some references.

He loved doing research, digging around to find the treasure that no one else had. It was what he liked about going to school. Figuring out a problem or finding the answer to a puzzle that no one else had fascinated him. It got him up in the mornings when sometimes it felt as though there was no reason.

Dayne put the copies he'd gathered into his computer bag in the trunk of his car and then got in and started for home. The freeway was clogged, and it took over half an hour to go the ten miles to his exit. From there he made good time and was able to reach his neighborhood fairly quickly. Dayne neared home, but a police vehicle at the end of his street blocked his way.

Pulling as close as he dared and rolling down the window, Dayne said, "I'm trying to get home. My house is down there." The smell of smoke filled the air, and he worried about his neighbors.

"There's a fire," the police officer said. "They're getting it under control."

Dayne pulled his car into the drugstore parking lot across the street, got out, and walked up to where a group of neighbors had gathered. He turned to where they were all looking and gasped as flames shot out of the windows of his little house.

"Oh God," Dayne mumbled as he hurried forward. Everything he owned was in that house. It was all he had left of his mom. As flames shot out of the front door and the roof collapsed, Dayne's legs gave out and the grass rose up to meet him.

"Hey," a deep voice said from close to him. Dayne felt like a fool and struggled to get up. He was helped to his feet, and the fireman took off his helmet. "It's you."

"That's my house…," Dayne said weakly as water sprayed all over what was left of the only home he'd known. "Everything I have…." He gasped and tried not to come apart at the seams.

"It will be all right." He took Dayne's arm and gently helped steady him.

"I don't see how." Everything was gone. The last of what he'd had from his mother had been in that house, and the flames had taken it all. A cloud of steam went up as the last of the fire died away, leaving only a smoking ruin of what had been his life. One of the walls fell in, and Dayne turned away.

"I'm sorry this happened to you." The firefighter gently put an arm around Dayne's shoulder, and the last of Dayne's control broke.

He buried his face in the man's chest and cried like the stupid baby he was. Damn it, he tried not to, but this was too much. For a year, he'd been doing his best to hold it together, to get through each day as it came, hoping the pain would lessen. But every damn time he thought things might be getting better, something happened, and this was one of the worst.

"It's all right. Just let it out."

Dayne heard people around him, but he kept his face where it was for a bit, afraid to look for fear of dying of embarrassment. Dayne breathed deeply and backed away, swallowing and getting himself together. "I'm sorry." He wiped his eyes and tried not to get snot all over himself.

"Don't be." The man didn't move, and Dayne lifted his gaze.

"I guess after I slobbered all over you, I should tell you my name. I'm Dayne." He wiped his hands on his pants because they were covered with things he shouldn't have on them.

"I'm Lawson Martin." He took Dayne's hand and held it.

This seemed normal and yet surreal. He was standing on his neighbor's lawn after watching almost everything he owned go up in flames, and when Lawson did something so ordinary, Dayne felt a little better. At least he didn't want to break down in tears again, though he'd probably do that later.

"I know this sounds trite, but things will be all right. You weren't home, and everything can be replaced except you."

"Somehow I doubt I'm irreplaceable." A tear ran down Dayne's cheek as he realized his life as he knew it was gone. Not that there was all that much to it.

Lawson frowned slightly. "That isn't the way to talk. Yes, things look bad, but you'll call your family or friends, and they'll be there to help you. Do you know your insurance company?"

That Dayne did know, and he reached into his pocket to pull out his phone. Of course, the battery was dead, and he groaned once again. "I guess I'll call them later."

Another fireman approached them, water dripping off his coat and pants. He removed his helmet, and Dayne sighed in relief. "Morgan," he said quietly. At least there was someone here he knew.

"I'm sorry. As soon as I heard the address, I knew it was your house, and we got here as fast as we could."

Dayne nodded. "I know you did." He looked at what was left of his home. It hadn't been much, just four rooms and a bath, but it had been his and, before that, his mom's. "Do you know what happened?"

"We think it was the wiring. There was a power surge about an hour ago, and I think it might have overloaded some of the circuits. They likely smoldered for a while and then caught fire."

"Oh." He sighed.

"I'll have the fire marshal's office send you a report for the insurance company. At least it was an accident, and your insurance can't give you any trouble about that."

"Thanks, Morgan." He heaved another sigh, not knowing what he was going to do.

"Do you and Lawson know each other?" Morgan asked, looking at them.

"We met this afternoon at the historical society." Lawson smiled. "He was doing some kind of research, and I was trying to find out something about my family. Apparently my grandfather's brother went to the Carlisle Indian Industrial School at one time, or at least that's the family story, but I can't find any record of him."

Dayne nodded. "It seems that they often changed or used anglicized versions of the students' names. That's my research project...." God, how was he going to manage to do everything now? "I was reading a few student journals, and two of them talked about it. So if the records referred to their student names but they went by their traditional names when they left, and if you don't know what the name was...." At least he was talking about something other than his shell of a house.

"I guess I figured that...." Lawson nodded slowly, as though he were admitting defeat.

"Do you have a place to stay tonight?" Morgan asked.

Dayne turned to where the neighbors had stood. They were filtering away, and even though Dayne had lived in the house for seven years, not one of them had offered to help him. That was probably his own fault. He wasn't an outgoing person, not since the accident. "I can go to a hotel. I have my car, and once I charge my phone, I can find a place to stay." He could tell that Morgan was ramping up to offer him a room, but Morgan and Richard had their hands pretty full at the moment, and he didn't want to be a bother. He'd get through this somehow.

"He can stay with me," Lawson said to Morgan. "I've got plenty of room, and it's already getting late."

"Don't you need to finish your shift?"

"I wasn't scheduled. They called me in because of the fire, and I came right over, but you were all taking care of it, and then I saw Dayne here and thought I'd try to help him."

Dayne sent up a silent thank-you that Lawson didn't explain how he'd blubbered all over him.

"We have room. It's just that with the remodeling...."

Dayne knew Morgan and Richard were reworking Morgan's house to better accommodate Richard's wheelchair. They lived just a block away and had become friends—some of the few he had in the neighborhood—mostly because Richard had made an effort to get to know Dayne when he was out on his rides around the area for exercise.

"Like I said, I have room."

"Excuse me...," Dayne said, then wished he hadn't, because he wasn't sure how to say what he wanted to without sounding snarky.

"Sorry. I guess we were talking right over you. That was my fault. Dayne, I have plenty of room at my house, and you can stay for a few days. It's three blocks over, so you won't be too far away."

"Dayne, Lawson's a really good man. I've worked with him for, what... two years now? You'll be well taken care of."

Dayne turned back to the shell of his home. "I don't have anything." He looked down at the clothes he was wearing. Other than the stuff in his trunk, which contained his computer and schoolbooks, that was it.

"Don't worry. We can get you what you need," Lawson said gently.

"I don't know what to do first."

"Okay. Then we'll get you to a store for a few essentials. We can charge your phone, and you can make your phone calls. You need to eat, and then you can go to bed and figure out the rest in the morning."

Dayne was so overwhelmed that he agreed. "Do they need anything from me?"

"Don't think so. We're just making sure everything is out, and then we'll pack up. There isn't anything more that can be done here tonight." Morgan motioned, and a man in a white shirt came over. "Cap, this is Dayne Mills. He's the owner."

"I'm sorry for what happened." He said it with such sympathy that Dayne nodded, and it was all he could do not to break down again.

"Do you need anything from him?"

"Not at the moment. We're finishing up. I'm sorry, but it looks like the house is a total loss. The fire marshal will have a report for you and your insurance company." Thankfully he didn't smile. "Are you the only occupant?"

"Yes. It was just me, and I didn't have any pets." He tried to look at that as a positive, but it only brought into greater clarity just how alone he actually was.

"Thank you." The captain didn't seem to know what else to say, and Dayne wasn't sure if there was anything else he should ask. All he wanted to do was find a hole somewhere, crawl into it, and try to grieve for all he'd lost.

"Why don't you let me take you to get what you need, and then we can get you settled?"

Dayne nodded, numbness spreading through him. Was he really going to go home with a stranger? He should probably just insist on getting a hotel room. He thought about his meager bank balance and figured the insurance company would pay for it in the end, but....

Morgan led him away from the others by gently placing a hand on his back. "You can come stay with Richard and me instead if you want... but the place is pretty torn up and...."

Dayne knew that wasn't a possibility. All the dust and construction debris would send his allergies into overdrive, and he'd spend the entire night wheezing. He'd have to medicate himself into oblivion just to try to remain breathing. "I don't know what to do."

"Lawson is a wonderful guy, and you have nothing to worry about."

Dayne released a huge breath. "Okay." It wasn't like he had many viable alternatives at the moment. He turned and walked back to where Lawson stood. "I really appreciate your offer. Thank you."

"Okay. Let's get you some stuff, and then we can go back to the house." Lawson motioned across the street to a brand-new Charger. He unlocked the car, walked to the passenger side, and opened the door for him. Dayne didn't know what to make of the gesture, but he got in the car and buckled his seat belt.

Lawson got in and started the car. He drove surprisingly carefully given the power that thrummed under the hood.

"Why would you do something like this?"

"Like what?"

Dayne shrugged. "Open your house to a complete stranger. That isn't in your job description, I'm sure."

Lawson's scoff turned to a laugh. "Honestly? I see people every day who lose everything they have to fire, including loved ones. They cry and they hold each other, but... shit, I shouldn't say any of this right now."

Dayne huffed and rolled his eyes. "Things can't get much worse."

Lawson made the turn into the shopping center and pulled up to the drugstore. Dayne got out and went inside. He picked out a shaving kit and then some basic things he would need—a razor, shaving cream, toothbrush, toothpaste. As he reached for his brand of deodorant, his hand began shaking, and he couldn't stop it. His eyes filled with tears, and he still quivered as he wiped them away.

"Is this all you need?" Lawson asked, suddenly behind him, and then he scooped Dayne into his arms. "It's all right."

"You keep saying that, but it doesn't feel like it's ever going to be all right again."

"It will be. Trust me." Lawson took the basket from his hand, and once Dayne was able to stand on his own again, Lawson carried it to the front. He was already paying and bagging the things by the time Dayne reached the counter.

"Please...."

"It's fine. Let's get you something to wear for tomorrow." Lawson handed him the bag of items and motioned for Dayne to go ahead of him.

Dayne left the store, and Lawson drove them to the nearby strip mall with a department store. Inside, Dayne picked out a few shirts and jeans, as well as new underwear and socks. He paid for them and carried the bag out to the car, and Lawson drove him back to his car.

"Just follow me to my house." Lawson waited for him, and Dayne followed the red Charger the few blocks to a two-story, redbrick house with a porch, white pillars, and pretty flowers everywhere. This wasn't what he'd expected. He'd been picturing a low-fuss, low-maintenance sort of place. This was anything but.

"It's beautiful," Dayne said as he got out of his car.

Lawson walked over and smiled. "I've always loved this house, so when it came on the market a few years ago, I bought it. The previous owners lived here for twenty years, and they did a lot of the landscaping. I've done my best to keep it up."

Richard pulled up in front of the house, and Dayne went to meet him. When he leaned into the car, Richard hugged him tightly.

"I'm sorry this happened." Richard held him for quite a while. "I know exactly how it feels."

"Richard!" Lawson called happily, his hands full of bags from Dayne's car. "Come on inside."

Dayne released Richard and pulled his chair from behind the seat. Richard slid into it and wheeled up the walk and around to the side door.

"Lawson added a ramp for me a few months ago. He wanted me to feel welcome when we visited."

The door opened, and Lawson stood waiting for them. Richard glided into the kitchen, and Dayne followed, looking around the bright, warm room. His mother would have loved this kitchen, with its rich cabinets and cheery cream walls and granite counters. This would have been a dream for her.

"Let's go to the living room," Lawson offered, waving them through. "I put your things up in the guest room. It's at the top of the stairs, first door on your right."

"Thank you." Dayne's adrenaline, which had been sustaining him for a while, was giving out. He sat on the sofa and sank into the cushions. God, it felt so good. "Did you feel lost after the fire?" he asked Richard.

"Yeah, I did. I had no idea what was going to happen to me." Richard looked down at his legs, and Dayne wished he hadn't said anything. "That was when I met Morgan again, and after that, things began getting better."

Lawson came in and pressed a cool glass into Dayne's hand. "I know you probably want a stiff drink, but I made some lemonade."

"With vodka in it?" Dayne didn't really drink much, but half a bottle of cheap vodka would probably be good right about now.

"That isn't going to help, and you'll only wake up tomorrow feeling worse." Lawson sat next to him on the arm of the sofa. "Do you like pasta? I have some red sauce, or I can make pesto."

Dayne's stomach rumbled. "Pesto...." He closed his eyes and did his best not to think about his mother's cooking. "Thank you."

To Dayne's surprise, Lawson gently patted his shoulder. "Did you need to charge your phone?"

"Oh God. I can't remember anything right now." Dayne jumped up and nearly spilled his drink, he was so scatterbrained. He set it on a coaster on the coffee table and hurried to his car. He got his computer bag and went back inside.

After asking Lawson which outlet he could use, Dayne got his phone plugged in. He returned to his seat on the sofa and felt himself sinking into his own thoughts. His eyes unfocused and he didn't move, just thinking and wondering what he was going to do next. His world was crashing down around him and had been for the last year. There had to be something he could do to stop the slide that seemed to have been going on for so long.

Lawson sat next to him on the sofa, and Dayne turned to him, jaw set. If Lawson said one more time that everything was going to be all right, Dayne wasn't sure if he could stop himself from hitting him. He didn't know where his anger was coming from, but it boiled up from deep inside. He clenched his fists and closed his eyes, trying to keep from flying into a million pieces as he waited for what everyone seemed to want to say.

Instead, Lawson wrapped his big arms around him and held him tight. The anger slipped away as quickly as it had built, and Dayne buried his face against Lawson's chest, holding him in return. "Sometimes words just aren't what's needed," Lawson whispered. "You take all the time you need. No one is going anywhere." He rocked slowly and rubbed Dayne's back.

It had been so long since anyone had been so nice to him. Over the last year, he had learned that loneliness ate at you from the inside and perpetuated itself. Sometimes he had longed for contact with others so badly that he was almost willing to make a fool of himself to get attention. Dayne didn't cry, which he was pretty proud of. He did soak in Lawson's warmth and attentiveness. He knew this was only because of the loss he'd suffered and because Lawson was trying to help him, but it felt nice to be held and looked after, even if the huge, handsome man felt sorry for him.

"Better?" Lawson whispered, and Dayne nodded slowly. "Good." Lawson released him and then slowly got to his feet. He moved the way Dayne imagined someone might around a skittish horse they didn't want to frighten. "Give me a few minutes and I'll finish up dinner." He left the room, and Richard leaned forward in his chair.

"Are you feeling more comfortable?"

"I guess." Dayne shifted on the sofa, because even while he was in shock, Lawson's hug had set his stupid dick to thinking things it shouldn't be thinking. He wanted to thump the damn thing and tell it to behave, but it didn't seem to want to listen, especially when it came to Lawson. "I appreciate you coming over." God, he hated playing the part of the damsel in distress. It really sucked.

"Your phone is probably charged enough that you can make some calls." Lawson handed it to him, and Dayne stared at the screen, trying to make his brain work.

"What company do you have?" Richard asked, taking the phone from him. When Dayne told him, he looked up their number, dialed it, and handed the phone back.

It took a few minutes to get through the phone system, but finally Dayne got to a live person. "Yes. There's been a fire at my home." He was asked all kinds of questions he didn't know the answers to, but eventually they got to his policy and he was able to tell them some basic information. They promised to have an adjuster call him soon. As soon as he hung up, his phone rang. "Hello?"

"Dayne? This is Kevin, Angus's partner. We met a few months ago at Morgan and Richard's cookout. Angus just told me what happened, and if you think of something you need, just let us know. You have my number on your phone, so just call if there's anything we can do."

"Thank you." Dayne was starting to wonder if he'd stumbled into some sort of underground fire victims' support group.

"Just know you aren't alone. Morgan and Richard and I know what you're going through." He sounded so positive and sincere. "Where are you now?"

"Lawson's. He's giving me a place to stay for the night."

"That's good. He's a cool guy. Just take it easy and try not to get overwhelmed."

"I'm trying, but it's hard."

19

"Angus has seen this a lot. He says it's a one-day-at-a-time kind of thing, and I have to agree with him. It was how he helped me." Kevin's tone shifted, still carrying some of his natural excitement but more serious. "I know everyone says this, but you'll figure it out and things will be okay. I know that doesn't make up for all the things you lost that can't be replaced—nothing can do that. Shit… I told myself I wasn't going to get maudlin."

"I think it's been that kind of day."

"Yeah, it has. But try not to stress over it, and know you have friends who can help you."

Dayne thanked him, and Kevin said good-bye and ended the call.

"Come on in for dinner," Lawson said, and Dayne waited for Richard and followed him into the kitchen. Lawson put Richard at one end of his small table, with Dayne sitting across from him. The pasta looked and smelled amazing, and as soon as Dayne took a bite, he realized just how hungry he was. His stomach was still a little reticent until the third bite, and then he turned ravenous. The food was good, and he hadn't eaten since his small lunch between classes.

"How long had you lived in the house?" Lawson asked.

"Seven years, I think. My mother saved for a long time so she could buy a house, and this one fit the two of us." He put down his fork. "The original plan was for it to be just her house. I had a job and was living on my own for a while, but then I had to move back in with her." He looked down at the food on his plate. He hadn't wanted to go there, but just about every conversation he had about himself led to his accident.

"You don't have to talk about it," Richard said, turning to Lawson, who nodded.

"I try not to dwell on it." The aftermath of his accident and the condition it left his legs in was a constant battle. He didn't need to make it dinner conversation as well. He saw the looks he got from passing strangers when he made his way down the street.

Lawson left the room and returned with Dayne's glass. He set it on the table. "Why don't you tell me some more about your research? Have you picked a specific topic for your paper or are you just starting out?"

Dayne wanted to hug him for changing the subject. "Right now I'm trying to find a topic. I really want to concentrate on the students and the school's impact on them, but I haven't found anything unique yet. I'm working on it, though. I was going through some diaries today, and a few of the students told some similar stories, so I may be able to start with that."

"Was the school a success?" Lawson asked.

"In some ways people thought it was, but in the end, it wasn't. By some accounts, 10,000 students attended the school over the years, but only 158 seemed to have graduated. That's a very poor rate."

"Why?" Lawson asked, clearly interested.

"I don't know." Never had saying those words in answer to a question brought a smile to his face. That could be his entire paper right there, and all it took was a single question.

"You're smiling," Lawson said with a grin of his own.

"You seem to have helped me come up with a topic for my paper. At least that's one question in my life answered." Now he just had to figure out what he was going to do with the rest of it.

Chapter 2

WOW, WHAT a strange and interesting day. Lawson sat next to Dayne and felt so sorry for him. Not that he wanted Dayne to know that. He didn't think Dayne wanted anyone's pity. He was just having one hell of a shit day. Now the adorable man was in his house, sitting at his table.

When Lawson had first seen him at the historical society, Dayne had pushed all his buttons. Lawson was a big guy—he knew that—and he had other large, muscular guys trying to get his attention all the time. But they didn't do it for him. Lawson figured he wanted what he wasn't, so slender guys with more delicate frames and spitfire blue eyes really got his motor running, especially if they had a hint of vulnerability and shyness. Basically, Dayne had caught his attention at the society, and when he'd seen him nearly collapse at the scene of the fire, he'd immediately sprung into action.

Not that he picked up vulnerable guys at fire scenes on a regular basis. That wasn't his thing either. But something about Dayne drew him in. Shit, maybe it was the fact that the guy really seemed to need some assistance.

"I'm glad I could help with the topic, and I'd like to read the paper when you're done. I'd like to learn more about my family. There's always been this mystique around town and within my family because Jim Thorpe went there. That seems to be all everyone remembers, so it's gotten glorified."

"Well, I'd be glad to send you a copy." Dayne ate more slowly, and Lawson refilled his glass. It was nice having company for a while. Dayne's phone rang, and he pulled it out of his pocket and turned away from the table. "Hello...?" he said tentatively and then listened. "Oh, thank goodness.... Yes, it was an accident. The fire marshal is putting together a report.... That will help a lot." The relief in Dayne's voice was palpable. "I have class until three tomorrow, so can I meet you at four?" He looked to be getting nervous again, running a hand through his hair. "Thank you. I'll see you then." Dayne hung up.

"The insurance adjuster?"

"Yes. He said he's going to meet me tomorrow and will have an initial check so I can start replacing some of the things I'm going to need immediately."

"That's good." Richard reached over to squeeze Dayne's hand.

A twinge of jealousy shot through Lawson. He knew Dayne and Richard were friends, but he wanted to be the one to comfort him. Lawson had just met the guy.... Okay, he was acting stupid, but it was still what he wanted.

"I know this is very difficult for you, but you have people who will help," Richard said.

"Thanks, both of you." Dayne finished eating his pasta, and the rest of the meal passed quietly.

Once they were all done with dinner, Richard said good night and headed out shortly afterward, leaving him and Dayne alone.

"Go on and have a seat in the living room if you want." Lawson disliked leaving dishes unwashed. With his job, he was often on shift for extended periods and hated coming home to a mess of any kind, so he always did a thorough cleanup. Once he was done, he got a couple of beers from the refrigerator, carried them into the living room, and offered one to Dayne.

"I keep wondering what I'm going to do." Dayne sighed. "I know the insurance company will figure out some value to the damage, and I can either rebuild the house or try to buy a different one, but that house had all my family pictures. I have a few on my computer, but they're recent. The ones my mom took of me as a baby are all gone, and I don't have any of her holding me. It's like that part of my life has been wiped away."

Lawson had meant to sit in his usual chair, but he took a seat on the sofa next to Dayne. "This may sound dumb, but the real important things are in here." He gently touched the center of Dayne's chest. "No one can ever remove her from your heart. And tomorrow, when you're supposed to meet the adjuster, I'll go with you if you like, and we'll see if anything can be salvaged. I've seen strange things survive fires. So you never know."

"You don't have to do that. You've been so nice to me already."

"There's been a fire, and that weakens what remains of structures. So I'll check around to make sure it's safe, and then we can see what we can find. I don't want you getting hurt."

"Why do you care so much? No one else does." He looked down at his lap, his expression sad.

"That's not true. Richard cares, and so does Morgan. Other people care too. So just give them a chance to help you." Lawson took Dayne's hand. "Why do you find it so hard to believe that you aren't alone?"

"I just do." Dayne pulled his hand away, opened the beer, and drank most of the bottle in one go.

"Slow down a little."

Dayne shook his head and seemed on the verge of talking, but remained quiet. Lawson was patient enough, drinking his beer, letting him work through his thoughts.

"You don't know what it's like," Dayne said quietly.

"What?"

"I lost my mom a year after I hurt my legs. My mom, my boyfriend at the time, Jeff, and I were on 581, and some guy was illegally hauling a trailer. It wasn't properly secured and broke loose from the car. It had safety chains, but he hadn't used them. The trailer was right ahead of us." Dayne shuddered, closing his eyes, and Lawson wanted to comfort him but sensed this wasn't the time. "The trailer swerved and the hitch must have dug into the pavement. It reared up and whipped around. Mom tried to avoid it, but it was too late. The trailer flew through the front of the car and...." Dayne sighed, opening his eyes. "It killed Jeff instantly and mangled the car around me before we came to a stop. I don't remember most of what happened. I woke up in the hospital with a neurosurgeon saying that he was going to try to save my legs."

Lawson didn't need to ask a bunch of questions to know how it went. Dayne still had his legs, but Lawson had also seen the pain he was in and his difficulties walking. "How long were you in the hospital?"

"Weeks, many weeks, and then there was physical therapy. I had my legs, but they said I might never be able to use them again. At first I didn't care, but then I thought that my mom would be alone and that Jeff wouldn't want me lying in a hospital bed, so I got up and fought to use them. It was months before I could go back to work, and even then there was pain. Jeff and I had gotten an apartment together, and we were talking about getting married. Then one asshole doesn't do what he's supposed to and Jeff is gone, my life is turned upside down forever, and I have to move back in with Mom because I need help."

Lawson leaned close and hugged him. "Do you have any idea how strong you are?"

"No, I'm not. I'm the guy who cried on your shoulder just a few hours ago."

"And you think that makes you weak?" Lawson released Dayne and stood, pulling up his shirt to expose his side. "I was in the academy doing practice drills when one of the other guys got turned around in the smoke. He slipped, carrying a fire ax. This was the result. It damaged the front of my hip, and I had to have surgery to graft in bone tissue."

"And you still became a fireman?" Dayne reached out and lightly touched the scar.

"It was all I ever wanted to do. They did surgery, and then another to fix what they missed the first time." Lawson lowered his shirt. "I understand what it takes to go through physical therapy and work through the pain. And that's strength. You may cry because of the pain—I've done it—but it's the will to keep going and the drive to get better that shows what's inside us." Lawson saw that strength in Dayne's eyes, and it was damned attractive.

"Thanks." Dayne gave him a little smile, which justified recounting one of the most difficult struggles in Lawson's life, though it didn't sound like it measured up to what Dayne had been through. But if sharing his experience helped Dayne feel better, then it was worth it. Dayne drank the rest of his beer and set the bottle on a coaster. Then he sat back on the sofa and closed his eyes.

"You look so tired. Come on. I'll show you the guest room." Lawson stood, and Tatianna decided to make an appearance from the other room.

"You have a cat?" Dayne asked, his eyes widening.

"Yeah. Are you allergic to her?"

"No." Dayne sat still as she wandered around the room. "Where has she been?"

"Tati doesn't come out when there are other people in the house." Lawson squatted, and she trotted over to him, meowing softly. "I'm surprised she came out now. I expected her to spend most of the night hiding since you're here." He petted her, and Tati rubbed against him. Then to his surprise, she wandered over to Dayne and rubbed around his feet.

"What's she doing?" Dayne sounded scared for some reason.

"She's saying hello. There's nothing to worry about. She doesn't attack or scratch. If she gets scared, she'll run out of the room."

Dayne unwound his arms from around himself and leaned forward, slowly extending his arm so he could touch her. She stilled, and Lawson figured Tati would bolt, but she stayed where she was, and Dayne gently stroked down her back. "You're a pretty girl, aren't you?" He continued petting her, and she wound around his legs again.

"That's a surprise. She really likes you." Lawson watched as Dayne sat back once again, and Tati jumped onto the sofa and pranced over to him and onto his lap. She rubbed against him and then jumped down and left the room, most likely to see what was in her bowl. "Did you have pets growing up?"

"No. Mom was allergic to everything, so I never had any animals. I asked about getting a snake once, and Mom freaked out, so I never asked for anything else." Dayne got off the sofa, and Lawson led him out of the room and up the stairs. "I always wanted a dog, but I could never have one." Dayne sniffled. "The shitty thing is that Jeff and I were on our way to a dog rescue. He'd contacted them, and they had a miniature beagle that we were planning to adopt."

Jesus. It seemed every time Dayne got close to getting what he wanted, something went to hell.

"I love animals. I only have Tati because she's really good about taking care of herself. The neighbor girl comes over on the days I work and makes sure she has food and is doing okay. Maryann is usually the only person besides me that she'll come out for."

Lawson pushed open the door to the bedroom. "There are towels on the dresser there, and the bathroom is right across the hall. Your things are on the bed, and you can feel free to use the television. The remote is on the nightstand."

"Thank you for everything. You didn't have to do any of this."

"I'm glad I can help. If you need anything, my room is the one at the end of the hall." Lawson walked out of the room, leaving the door cracked. He wasn't particularly tired, but he went downstairs to turn off the lights. He thought about watching television, but didn't want to disturb Dayne, so he locked everything up and went back upstairs.

Water ran in the bathroom, and Lawson imagined Dayne in the shower for about a minute and then wanted to slap himself for perving on the guy after the day he'd had. Lawson continued down to his room, undressed, cleaned up, and got ready for bed. He climbed between the sheets, turned out the lights, and flipped on the television to find something mindless to watch, listening in case Dayne needed anything. The house was quiet, and eventually Lawson turned off the television and rolled over to sleep.

LAWSON HAD no idea what time it was or why he was awake, but something wasn't right. He sat up, listening, and heard a cry. He shoved back the covers and followed the whimpers and cries to Dayne's room. Hearing a "No!" Lawson peered inside.

Dayne had kicked off the covers, his eyes still closed, and was lying on his side, kicking his legs repeatedly. Lawson was about to turn to leave when Dayne cried out once more and lurched toward the edge of the bed. Lawson raced forward and caught him as he came off the mattress. Dayne struggled and fought, squirming and thrashing.

"Dayne, it's all right." He laid Dayne back on the bed and gently tried to wake him.

"Lawson?" Dayne asked, instantly calming and looking up at him with startled blue eyes. "What are you doing here?" He grabbed for the covers at the end of the bed and yanked them up to cover himself. Then Dayne looked back at him, and even in the light from the hall, Lawson saw Dayne blush beet red and then turn away.

"You were thrashing, and I caught you as you fell off the bed." Lawson took a step back so he didn't cause Dayne any more distress. "I heard you yelling in your sleep and wanted to make sure you were okay." God, did Dayne think he was attacking him or something?

"Oh." Dayne relaxed a little and lowered the covers he'd been using like a shield. "I guess I'm a little jumpy."

"Ya think?" Lawson teased, giving Dayne a wink. Thankfully Dayne understood and smiled slightly. Lawson sat on the edge of the bed. "Do you want to talk about what happened?"

"It's the middle of the night and…." Dayne's eyes darted around the room, settling on him for a few seconds and then moving away. "You're nearly naked," he finally squeaked out, and Lawson realized he was only wearing a pair of old boxer shorts.

"I didn't mean to make you uncomfortable. I was just concerned when I heard you calling out." As he went to stand, Dayne touched his arm. Lawson stilled when Dayne didn't move his hand or pull away.

"You're stunning," Dayne breathed, then turned away, pulling his hand back. "Sorry. That was a dumb thing to say." He raised the shield of covers again. "Just let me die of embarrassment here. You've been nice enough to let me stay here. You don't need some twiggy doofus perving on you."

Lawson reached for Dayne, touching his chin with just the tips of his fingers. "How about I go back to bed, and we both try to get some more sleep? I understand if you don't want to talk about what's happening, but try to sleep and not fall off the bed. I don't want you to hurt yourself." Dayne's lips, red and pulled slightly with worry, screamed irresistible, and his eyes were filled with such pain that Lawson wanted to kiss it all away. He knew it wasn't that simple—pain and loss rarely were, especially with as much as Dayne had endured lately—but he wanted to try.

Dayne gazed at him, and Lawson saw Dayne's hands and arms relax, the covers lowering enough to reveal where his nipples poked slightly at the fabric of his T-shirt. Damn, Lawson wanted to tug away that cotton and reveal what was underneath. Heat built in his groin, and he needed to cool it or things were going to get awkward, and he wasn't wearing enough to keep his dick from making a full-on appearance. Not that he was ashamed of what he had in any way, but he didn't need to scare Dayne or have Dayne think he was trying to push himself on him. "Good night," Lawson rasped, lightly caressing Dayne's cheek before standing and leaving the room.

As Lawson returned to his room, Tati came up the stairs. She sat, blinking at him the way cats did, and Lawson looked back. At some point in the night, she usually paid him a visit. Lawson expected her to stroll over, but instead she slinked across the hall, peeked into Dayne's room, and went inside. He watched, and she didn't come out. Sneaking back, he peered through the open door. Dayne lay on his side, facing away from the door, with Tati curled in the crook of

29

his legs, her back pressed to Dayne's backside. Lawson shook his head, returned to his room, and went back to bed, trying not to think of Dayne.

"HEY, SHIRL, what's going on?" Lawson answered through his car's Bluetooth as he drove.

"Dennis and I are going up in the plane, and a spot opened up. We were wondering if you wanted to take a jump. We have a class taking their first solo jumps."

Lawson's heart immediately beat faster as adrenaline pumped through him at the thought of it. But then he sobered. "Sounds great. But I can't today. A friend's house burned yesterday, and I'm helping him look for anything that might be left. You all have fun and think of me as the ground rushes up at you." He grinned. That was the part that always got his blood pumping. The earth racing closer, him going faster and faster as it approached, and then popping the chute, pulling up, and watching until he kissed the ground. It was a real rush, and Lawson lived for that feeling of being truly alive.

"All right. But soon."

"You got it." He smiled as he hung up, but it faded as he made the final turn.

Lawson pulled up to the remains of Dayne's home a half hour before he expected Dayne to arrive. As he got out, the scent of charred wood, ash, and water hung in the air. There wasn't much left of the structure except parts of the exterior walls. Lawson walked across the lawn and up to what was left of the front of the house. He peered inside at the debris-laden floor and wondered if it had survived. He walked around to the back of the house and got his answer. Large holes indicated the floor had given way in parts. Sometimes basements would remain intact and things could be salvaged from there, but it looked like the fire had been hot enough to reach deeply into the house.

The tiny garage on the alley, detached from the house, seemed to be in one piece. Some of the paint on the side facing the house had blistered, but that was it. Granted, Lawson doubted any of the things that were really important to Dayne had been stored in the garage, but at least something was whole. He returned to the house and carefully went in through the front, checking that parts of the floors were solid.

A car pulled up, and Lawson backed out and turned as Dayne walked haltingly across the yard.

"Is there anything at all?"

"Not that I can see," he said as an Explorer parked behind Dayne's car. "Go meet with the adjuster, and I'll look around some more." The heartbroken look on Dayne's face stabbed Lawson in the gut. Everything about Dayne got to him, and not just in a sexy way. Lawson knew he was hot; guys told him that all the time, especially when he used to go to one of the clubs downtown with Angus and Morgan. He hadn't done that in quite a while, though. Still, he knew he turned heads, and Dayne… he was different.

Lawson stole a glance to where the two men talked. Dayne stood tall and spoke earnestly. That inner strength he didn't seem to think he had was making itself known, and damn if that wasn't sexy as hell. Lawson turned away before Dayne saw him looking, deciding he'd try to get into the basement.

He found the stairs, which seemed to be in one piece, though charred and probably soaked with water. Lawson went back to his car, popped open the trunk, and grabbed a flashlight. He returned to the stairs, pushed away the debris with his feet, and descended slowly, shining his light around.

The back portion of the basement was a mess, with ash and charred boards and debris piled under where the floor had given way. He wasn't going to go very far because he didn't know how stable the remaining structure was. The scent of fire and burned wood increased as he stepped farther inside.

The floor seemed to have given way in the bedrooms. The remains of the rest of the house lay sprawled over the openings, with piles of more debris underneath. The far side of the basement seemed intact, with many of the items that had been on what Lawson guessed had once been plastic shelves and their contents melted beyond recognition. Other things lay scattered and covered in ash. There might be some things down here that could be salvaged.

Lawson turned his attention to the piles of debris, shining the light over them. He'd seen strange things in the aftermath of a fire, but this was indeed unusual. He turned to another one, which was shorter and longer, blinking in disbelief. What he'd thought were debris piles were dressers, charred and burned, but standing in the basement after having fallen through when the floor gave way. The damn things must be heavy as hell, but there they were.

Creaking above sent Lawson back to the stairs. He got out and breathed in fresh air as he strode to where Dayne stood with the adjuster. "How's it going?"

Dayne was wound tight and shaking. *What the hell?*

"We just need the official report to prove that no arson was involved, and then I can start the claim process."

Lawson wanted to smack the guy. "I'm Lawson Martin with the West Shore Fire Department, and we don't believe that arson was involved. It seems to have been an electrical issue brought on by a power surge."

"We have procedures, and I need to follow them." The guy was a real asshole. He was supposed to be helping Dayne, not giving him a hard time. "I can't issue anything until I know for sure that this was an accident."

Lawson growled and pulled out his phone. "Angus."

"Yeah, buddy?"

"Have you finished that report for Dayne Mills? I'm over at the house with him, and the insurance agent is being a dick on wheels." He met the man's gaze and loved how he colored.

"I have it down. I was at the house this morning and confirmed it. The electrical shorted out probably due to the surge. I found the root cause. It was an accident. Do you want me to talk to him?"

"Don't know if you really want to." Lawson handed the adjuster his phone.

The man spoke to Angus for a minute and then handed the phone back. "I have regulations that I have to follow, just like everyone else. The fire marshal is sending me a copy of the report directly." He opened the folder he was holding, pulled out a check, and handed it to Dayne.

Lawson glanced at it. The amount was pathetic, just a few hundred dollars. How was that going to help Dayne?

"Start making lists of the things in the house. Go room by room. You have replacement value on the house and the contents. Once I get the fire report, I'll get the claim processing started." He shook hands with Dayne and then walked back to his car.

"What an ass," Lawson growled as soon as he was gone.

Dayne stared at the check. "What am I supposed to do with this?" He waved it around. "It will pay for a few changes of clothes and maybe two nights in a hotel, and then…." He grew silent, stomping around the yard, waving his arms all around. "Those bastards," he swore and then stomped back to where Lawson stood, letting him get it out. "I need help and this is what they give me?"

"The report is already on its way. You heard Angus get an e-mail address. So he'll get it sent over and then things will start."

"But to act this way? I lost my home, and they practically accused me of setting the fire." The wind left Dayne's sails quickly, and he sighed. "I'll make it through somehow. I always do."

"You can stay at the house for a few more days, so don't worry about that."

"I can't impose on you." Dayne turned toward what was left of his house and grew quiet. After a few seconds, his shoulders shook slightly. Lawson gave him his privacy and left him alone to grieve a little. "I barely know you and you're being so nice." Dayne wiped his eyes and turned back around.

"I liked having you, and so did Tati. You're good company, and you're welcome to stay. I don't have to go back on shift for another couple of days, so make yourself at home and stop worrying about where you're going to stay."

"Okay. Thank you." Dayne's mood seemed to lift, and he managed a small smile.

"I may have some good news for you. The garage seems untouched, so whatever was in there survived. The basement got pretty hot, and the shelves and stuff melted down there."

"We didn't have much in the basement anyway. Sometimes when the water got high, it would get damp, so we didn't use it to store a lot of stuff."

Lawson led Dayne to the basement steps. "Just stay here, and I'll hand up what I think is salvageable." Lawson went back down the stairs and over to one of the dressers. He yanked, and the top drawer slid out. The front was a sooty mess, but inside, the clothes were dry. It looked like Dayne's mother's things. He carried the drawer back up the stairs and handed it to Dayne. "Set it on the lawn. I'm going to try to bring up more."

"How?" Dayne took it, staring.

"The dressers were heavy wood and fell through the weakened floor." Lawson got the next two drawers and brought them to Dayne and then cleared off the other dresser and carried the six drawers out. He also checked in the back, but everything there was a melted mess, and he wasn't sure he could get anything out of it now. He left the basement and reentered the fresh air, coughing and sneezing to get the burned scent and taste out.

"I can't believe these survived."

"They were heavy enough, and the wood was hard enough that the floor weakened and caved in under them before they burned through."

"I guess." Dayne raced to his car, opened the trunk, and grabbed some cloth grocery bags. He returned and shoved his clothes in them. Lawson got some from his car as well, and they were able to empty the drawers of Dayne's clothes. It was the first time he'd seen Dayne smile and show actual excitement since the historical society.

Dayne pointed to his mother's drawers. "Most of what's in there I should have thrown out long ago. I just never had the heart." He shrugged. "I pretty much closed off Mom's room and left it. I guess that's one chore the fire took care of for me." Lawson figured Dayne was trying for levity, but it seemed forced, though Lawson smiled a little. Dayne was trying, and Lawson knew this was damn hard for him. "I should have brought some trash bags."

"I think I might have some. Often after a fire my clothes stink so bad that I put them in plastic when I take them home so I don't trail the smell everywhere. They'll stink like char and smoke, but we can take the salvageable things to Goodwill. At least it will help someone." He should have gotten the bags before, but hadn't thought of it. He retrieved the roll from his trunk and let Dayne sort through the clothes.

"Oh my God," Dayne gasped as he pulled a couple of small boxes out of the bottom of one of the drawers. "These earrings were my mom's. She used to wear them when I was young." He ran over, vibrating with excitement. "My mom said this was a gift that my father gave her when they were in high school."

"What happened to him?"

"Mom said he joined the military, and they'd planned to get married when he came home. He was killed in the Gulf War. I never knew him. But Mom used to wear this all the time—and then she didn't anymore. I thought she might have lost it, but here it is." Dayne hurried back and went through what was in the drawers, which became a treasure hunt. He found a few pictures that made his lower lip tremble and another couple of boxes. That was it. A small pile of mementos. Dayne sorted the last of his mother's clothes and placed the stuff he was going to donate in the garbage bags. The rest he put on the street for the trash man. "I think I've had enough."

"Then let's go back to the house. We can start washing your clothes." It had been a hard day for him as well, and some quiet time would probably be good.

He loaded his trunk with what he could and waited until Dayne had everything he wanted, and they drove to his house. Lawson took the laundry to the basement, got a load going in the washing machine, and then joined Dayne upstairs.

He found Dayne on the sofa, a notebook next to him, reading an old browned book, with Tati curled in his lap. "Man, you have a real friend."

Dayne lowered what he was reading. "She's a sweetheart." He gently patted down her head and back, and she stretched and closed her eyes as though Dayne was now her own personal throne. "Is there anything I can do to help?" he asked, setting the book down. "It's so nice of you to let me stay, and you don't need to do everything for me. I can help."

"I was about to order a pizza and call it a night. What do you like on it, and do you want a beer?"

"I like meat on my pizza, and I would love a beer." Dayne moved to get up, and Her Highness reluctantly got off his lap. As soon as he stood, she curled up in the spot where Dayne had been sitting. Tati loved anywhere warm.

"Just relax. I have everything under control. Let me order the pizza and I'll sit with you." Lawson left the room and placed the order. When he returned with the beers, Dayne was back in his place with Tati right back on his lap.

"Listen to this…."

"What is it?"

"A diary of a student at the Indian school. It's dated September 8, 1908."

"I arrived today and know no one. At home with my tribe, I know everyone and am never alone. The other new students on the train were as scared and confused as I was. They milled around, looking abandoned. I was taught English and speak it well, but many of the others don't, and all the noise has to be terrifying. No one knew what to expect, and it frightened all of us. It seemed we had all heard the same rumors. After arriving and being taken from the station,

we were transferred to a wagon, each of us holding the single bag we were allowed on our laps. The road was rough and the wagon rocked badly. One of the younger boys got sick over the side, but they didn't stop. I moved next to him, gave him the last hard candy from my mom, and put an arm around him to comfort him. I know he cried into my shirt, but I let him have his dignity and kept the others from pointing at him. We rode over a rutted but less rough road to a large white building and were told that was the end of our journey. They called it our new home, but I swore that building or any of the others would never be home. I know where my home is, even if I am separated from it.

"We were each given a bed in the building, with a place to put the few things we'd brought. I was relieved that I wasn't going to be sleeping alone. My room is very small, with only one other person in it. I have always had people around me. It will be strange to not share a bed, but they are small, so I should be all right. I have a window that overlooks the grounds, so I can at least see outside.

"It turned out we didn't need what we brought because today I received White man clothes that itch and make my skin feel like there are bugs under it. How can they wear clothes like this? Is their skin so dead, they do not feel it? They gave me boots of leather and took my moccasins. My feet hurt and they can't be free. They still ache. I don't know how I'm going to walk tomorrow.

"I am a warrior. I will survive."

Dayne turned the page. "What surprises me is how articulate he is for a teenager." He returned to the diary.

"September 9, 1908

"They cut my hair so I look like a White man. I don't know how my tribe will recognize me when I return home. They said my hair will be cut every month, but my neck and head will freeze in the winter, and I begged them to let me keep it. Some of the younger boys cried, and I know their loss, but I stayed strong and will try to help them through their pain.

"I heard them last night as well, crying and scared in their beds, with no one to help them. The people at the school seem intent on making sure everyone is stripped of their tribal identity and belonging. It seems so harsh to me. I'm a warrior. I understand hurt and the need to be strong. These are young boys who haven't had a chance to learn such lessons and probably never will if they stay here. I want to help them and don't know how.

"When they were done, I left the hut where they do the cutting and ran into the woods. I needed to be alone with the spirits of the trees, but they do not recognize me either. Maybe these are strange trees who have lost their ability to speak. Maybe they are scared of the White men and have become silent, or they have forgotten their own language, just like the White man wants us to forget ours. We are forbidden to speak in our own language and must only use English. We are to be made gentlemen. I don't want to be whatever this gentleman is. I want to be myself, but I am not allowed to here.

"After my hair was removed, I was told that I had to have an English name. They call me Ted after the President of the United States, but I do not like it. I want to use my own name, the name my tribe gave me, but they punished Little Bird for using his, so I keep quiet and only hold my name in my heart. They can say what they want, but I know who I am and I will hold on to it. But the others don't have that to hold on to, and some walk around blankly, as though they are shells of themselves. I will help them even if I get in trouble here.

"I am a warrior. I will survive."

Lawson swallowed hard as the words sank in. His great-great-uncle had gone through that exact same treatment. The few stories he'd heard told of his uncle indicated he would have been about fifteen or sixteen at the time—the same age as Ted. Just thinking about having everything taken away like that sent Lawson's blood racing. The injustice and cruelty of it hit him hard.

Dayne lowered the diary, resting it on his lap. "I think I feel a little like him right now. Except I'm not…. I lost my home and the things in it, but I'm still me."

38

"Do you know his real name?" Lawson asked, still thinking of his great-grandfather's brother. In a strange way, he felt a connection to him he hadn't before.

"No. I think he's being cautious about it. From what I've read, the school believed that what was holding the Native Americans back was the fact that they weren't civilized, and since everything Anglo-European was considered civilized, they had it forced upon them." He sighed softly. "Just when I think shit is bad for me, I see someone who had it worse. Could you imagine being sixteen and having everything you know and understand ripped away from you?"

"Honestly, no." Lawson tried to get his thoughts around it and failed miserably. "I know who I am and what I like. My teenage years were hard enough, trying to figure myself out and why I was different. I can't imagine being thrown into a strange world where I understood even less."

"Neither can I." Dayne set the book aside when the doorbell rang, and Lawson went to grab the pizza.

Chapter 3

THEY ATE dinner in the living room. Lawson turned on the television, and they watched part of the latest Star Wars movie, but paused it for breaks to change the laundry and for Dayne to fold his things once Lawson brought them up.

Dayne still had homework to do, so he excused himself and went up to his room to get his books. He read through the material for his classes and then pulled the diary from his pack. Beverly had been good enough to let him take the book from the society, and he wanted to return it as soon as possible. He climbed onto the bed, propped his head up with the pillows, and continued reading. Most of the entries were rather normal, given the context. Ted seemed to get used to his new clothes, but he still disliked them. He joined one of the sports teams, and from his accounts, that seemed to provide an outlet and a connection to the outdoors that he needed.

"Do you need anything?" Lawson asked, setting a basket of laundry inside the door. "The last load is in the dryer."

"I'm good. Thank you." He marked his page with a piece of paper and closed the book. "I keep thinking about Ted. I know this is just one person's account, but his feelings leap off the page. He was miserable."

Lawson sat on the edge of his bed. "Let me ask you something. Why do you think he stayed? I'm assuming there are a lot more entries, so he didn't just pack up and go back home."

"How would he get there?"

Lawson smiled, and Dayne knew there was some idea behind it. "This is a man who was taught to live off the land, and if he came

40

from a reservation, he walked wherever he needed to go. Either that or he used a horse. He simply would have walked home. It might have taken weeks or months, but people did that. Remember, people walked across the entire country during the westward migration. So he stayed even though he could have left. Obviously lots of students did leave."

Lawson leaned a little closer, and Dayne got a whiff of him and tried not to let it short-circuit his brain. He smelled slightly of char from when they'd visited the house, but under that, a musky richness tickled at the back of Dayne's mind. He sat up, leaning in just to get another breath of him.

Dayne knew he was being super foolish. Lawson was as hot as hot could possibly get. He'd seen Lawson with his shirt off, and just thinking about it was enough to make Dayne's mouth water. Lawson was being nice to him and taking pity on him because he had lost just about everything. "I guess you're right." He pulled his thoughts back to their conversation and away from what he couldn't have. "And I haven't found the answer yet. I hope to."

"What answers do you want?" Lawson asked.

It took Dayne a few seconds to figure out what Lawson was asking, and even after that, he still wasn't quite sure how to answer. "You're going to have to help me here."

"We all have questions—the big questions. 'Why are we here?' and 'what's the meaning of life?' type questions. But there isn't any big, grand vision or some overarching plan. I think people exist because of some evolutionary lottery that made us possible."

"I don't think I was expecting such weighty questions. What do I want answers to?" He repeated Lawson's question, hoping some great answer would bubble up. "I don't know. Maybe why all this shit keeps happening to me?" His leg chose that particular moment to throb, and he jumped a little at the ache.

Dayne rubbed his right leg, and Lawson leaned closer. "Lie back and let me."

"That isn't necessary," Dayne croaked, but Lawson eased him down and gently rubbed his leg through his jeans.

The pain rippled once again, and he gritted his teeth. Lawson continued massaging, and Dayne let out his breath as his muscles relaxed and the pain eased back. "That's better," Lawson breathed, and Dayne tried like hell not to think too much about where Lawson's hands were going. "Just relax. It's been a trying couple of days and you're carrying a lot of tension here. That's probably why you're aching."

"It does that." Dayne shrugged, attempting to loosen up.

"Have they told you why?"

"My knees were damaged, and there were some breaks that didn't heal as well as we'd all hoped they would. On top of that, the muscle damage was pretty severe. So as you can see, I'm able to walk, but the muscles aren't particularly happy about it." Dayne pressed his head deeper into the pillow. "Oh God, that's so good." He sighed as the tension he'd been holding for months finally let go. "How do you know how to do this?"

Lawson chuckled. "Firefighters don't just learn how to throw water on burning buildings. We take a lot of classes in first aid and anatomy, since we're often the first ones on the scene of an accident."

Dayne groaned as Lawson's magic fingers slid up his thigh, finding just the place that held the last source of pain in his right leg. Part of him wanted Lawson to keep going, and he imagined what would happen if he did. Slipping open Dayne's jeans and sliding them off his legs—maybe he'd even like what he saw— Lawson would press his face to his skin.... Dayne returned to reality, and the heat in his groin retreated as quickly as it had risen.

Lawson was only being nice, nothing more. If he actually saw Dayne's legs, it wasn't likely he'd be rubbing them like that. There were times when Dayne looked at his legs in the mirror and cringed. The scars were much better now than they had been after the accident. Then it had been hard for him to see them, and he'd worn pants, even to bed. He didn't do that any longer, but he rarely looked closely at his legs. The scars served as yet another reminder of what he'd lost.

Dayne jumped slightly when Lawson touched a sensitive scar. "Did I hurt you?"

"No." It was hard to explain that sometimes his scars sent weird signals to his brain, especially when he wasn't expecting to be touched, and with his thoughts wandering, he'd been taken a little by surprise.

Lawson gentled his movements and then pulled his hands away. Dayne immediately missed the touch and wanted to ask Lawson for more. It had been so long since hands, other than his own, had touched him in any meaningful way. But he had no right to ask Lawson to continue to touch him, to hold him.

Tati jumped on the bed, wandered over the covers, rubbed against Lawson, and then bounded over to him to slide her head along Dayne's arm before curling into a ball next to him.

"I didn't realize how comforting pets could be." He stroked her back and wished…. He wanted so many things to be different in his life, but he didn't know how to make them happen.

"They seem to know when you're hurting and need comfort." Lawson met his gaze, and Dayne tried to figure out what it meant.

He nodded slowly. "I don't know what I'd have done if you hadn't helped me." He turned away and continued stroking Tati's silky fur. She felt so sleek and soft sliding beneath his palm. "I probably could have gotten a hotel, but… I know I'm going to have to find a place more permanent to live, and I'm thinking I'll see if there's anywhere closer to school, at least until the semester is out. I stayed in this neighborhood because that's where the house was, and I commuted, but I don't have to do that any longer."

"Why not take your time and think about it? You don't have to make any decisions at the moment. Tati and I are happy to have you here. I bought this house because I loved it, but I

didn't realize just how big it was until I started living here alone."
Lawson patted the bed and then stood and walked to the door. "I'll
see you in the morning. I'm not on shift tomorrow, but I have to
do a bunch of errands." He paused, looking at Dayne, and then
turned to leave.

"Lawson."

He turned back.

"Thanks." Dayne rubbed his legs and smiled. "They feel
better than they have in a long time." In truth his legs tingled only
a little.

"Anytime." Lawson left, and Dayne grabbed his bookbag from
next to the bed and finished his reading before cleaning up, getting
ready for bed, and turning out the light.

HIS DREAMS woke him in the dark, leaving him gasping for air. He'd
seen doctors who had told him that the dreams would most likely fade
over time, that they were the result of the extreme trauma he'd been
through. He hadn't had them in a while, and he expected the fire had
triggered their return. He listened and was thankful he hadn't woken
Lawson. The house remained quiet. Tati blinked at him and laid her
head back on the bedding. But he was awake and didn't think he'd be
going back to sleep soon.

Dayne turned on the light, thinking he'd get some more reading
done. He reached for his book bag and meant to pick up one of his
textbooks, but his hand closed around the spine of the journal. He
pulled it out and began reading.

October 4, 1908

*I saw him again today. I know what they call him here, Matthew,
and he hates his White man name just as much as I do. The White men
say we are not supposed to say such things, but he is strong and taller
than most. He has black hair and walks as stiffly and carefully in his
boots as I do. I still do not like them!*

44

Matthew is on the baseball team with me, and he's a real hitter and runs fast, but not faster than me. I run like the wind, and when I run, I picture that I'm racing away from all the White men, not stopping until I reach my village. We talked after practice, and I think it could be nice to have a friend. This place is lonely and so strange. Everything we do is designed to make us forget who we are and fill our heads with White men knowledge.

I'm getting used to some of the things here. The clothes don't itch as much as they used to, but I still miss my moccasins. I got some leather from one of the other guys and made myself a new pair at night when no one else could see me. I keep them hidden so no one finds them. I can't wear them much, but they remind me of home and make my feet happy.

October 5, 1908

I got into trouble today. After classes I came back to my room and saw the headmaster standing by my bed. I thought he might have found my moccasins and was afraid he'd taken them. That wasn't it. He'd heard me speaking Apache to Matthew, who is having trouble speaking English. At first I thought I was to be punished, but he said he wanted me to help the other Apache learn English. They need help.

The White men act like they know everything, how to act, what is right. And they need my help.

I am still trying to decide if this is good or another punishment the White man is pushing on us. Helping the others only pushes them further from their tribes. We need to talk in our own tongue and remember who we are. I have to hide this now. I'm writing things no one else can see. I know what's in my heart. They can dress me any way they like. I am a warrior, and no one can take that away from me.

Dayne blinked as he read the passage. He understood what it felt like to have everything he cared about taken away. And sometimes the loneliness and fear that Ted described loomed over Dayne like a shadow threatening to swallow him whole.

"You okay?" Lawson asked from the doorway, rubbing his eyes. "Did you have another nightmare?"

"Yeah. I had them after the accident for a long time, and eventually they mostly went away. I keep reliving it, except now the car bursts into flames around me."

"Do you need to get some help?"

"I've had it. I know what causes the dreams, and I know they'll fade again eventually. They scare me when they're happening, but when I wake up now, I know it was just a dream."

Lawson came into the room, wearing just a pair of sleep shorts that left little to the imagination, and sat on the bed. Dayne swallowed hard and turned away, but not for long. The view was way too good to pass up. "You were really thrashing last night."

"I know, and I'm sorry for freaking out like I did. I don't know you very well, and you were nearly naked and holding me and…." His cheeks heated. "I guess I was a little scared after the dream and let my imagination get the better of me."

"It's all right. I can understand how you'd react the way you did. I just didn't want you to fall and hurt yourself. You've been through a lot, and…."

"I'm okay. You've been a big help, and there are people who have things worse off than I do. The house is insured, and yeah, I can't replace some of the things in it, but I have to move on, right? I can't sit here, wallowing in a sea of self-pity." He indicated the book. "His name's Ted, and he went through worse than me. They were trying to take away his sense of self and identity. I know who I am, and I see myself pretty clearly."

Lawson crossed his arms over his strong chest, pressing his pecs deliciously forward. "What is it you see?"

Dayne chuckled. "I know I'm not the luckiest guy in the world or the best-looking, and what few looks I had, I lost in the accident. I know that. I'm trying to go to school so I can have a better future. There are some days I can barely walk, and even when I can, I look like some sort of demented penguin because my knees don't function very well. I know I'm not going to turn anyone's head, and I can live with that." Dayne shrugged.

"You know, you're so far off."

"Why? I don't have a ton of people beating a path to date me."

"Have you been open to dating? Have you gone anywhere to meet people?"

Dayne groaned softly. "Please. I went to my last class and I heard a guy talking to the one next to him, asking why he'd never seen the cripple around campus before if I was taking such high-level classes. That's how people see me, as the crippled guy who can't walk very well and sometimes needs a cane. I know that, and I can live with it."

"Really? You like people referring to you that way?" Lawson looked down his magnificent nose at Dayne. "When you hear something like that, it doesn't make you want to kick their ass?"

"Of course it does," Dayne countered, more forcefully than he intended, and the words poured out of him. "Let's see how that goes, shall we? I yell, or do what I really want and punch the ignorant bastards in the face, and they run away or kick my feeble legs from under me and beat the shit out of me. So I ignore it and go on. If they get a rise from me, then they've won, and I may be quiet, but I still like to win."

"Sometimes taking the high road sucks."

"Tell me about it." Dayne sometimes didn't know how much of it he could stand.

"But I still think you're wrong. You don't see yourself the way others do. Sure, some people see just the limp and your leg, but not everyone does. Some people see more. You need to give them a chance."

"How?"

"You think you have everything all figured out, and maybe you do. But what if you're wrong?" Lawson leaned closer, a wave of heat rolling off him. Dayne was relieved the covers over his lap hid his

47

reaction to Lawson's proximity, as the hot view that kept coming into greater relief was right in front of him.

"Who's going to want me?" Dayne blinked and met Lawson's stare. He hadn't honestly meant to challenge him, but that's what it sounded like.

Lawson slid his warm hand behind Dayne's neck, drew him closer, and kissed him.

Dayne was so surprised, he almost forgot to kiss back, and then he worried Lawson might think he was some sort of dead-fish kisser, so he returned the kiss. It ended too quickly, with Dayne blinking when Lawson pulled away. "What was that?"

"A kiss?"

"Was that you trying to make your point? Some pity kiss?" He narrowed his eyes, his brow furrowing.

Lawson scoffed and rolled his eyes. "I never do anything out of pity."

"Then why'd you kiss me?"

"Is it so strange that I might find you attractive and that I wanted to kiss you? I know you have this thing with questions, because you sure ask a lot of them. But that isn't the exact reaction I was hoping for." Lawson pursed his lips slightly. "I mean, the guys I kiss usually like it and want to do it again."

"So you kiss a lot of guys?"

"That isn't the point. If you don't want a repeat, that's fine. I just thought...."

"It was a really nice kiss," Dayne said quietly. "I didn't mean to act like I didn't like it. It's just that... why would you kiss me?"

Lawson shook his head. "Maybe I think you're cute."

Now it was Dayne's turn to scoff.

"So you think I let every guy I meet at the historical society or at a house fire come home with me?" He glared at Dayne and then smiled. "I like you. You were interesting and, yeah, a little vulnerable, and I definitely thought you were cute."

"I'm cute?" Dayne wasn't sure if he liked that idea or not. After thinking for a second, he decided he'd take cute. "You think I'm cute."

He smiled, still doubting Lawson would feel that way if he saw his legs. Dayne looked down at himself. He'd never thought of himself as cute, not even when he was a child.

"Yeah, and you're a bit of a spitfire."

"What I am is a mess."

Lawson caressed his cheek. "No, you're not. You're a guy who's had some difficult times, and I like to think that trying times can't last forever and good things are around the corner."

"Maybe." Dayne leaned closer, hoping Lawson would get the hint. He did, moving in and kissing him even harder. This time Dayne was ready and wound his arms around Lawson's neck, then let his hands slide down his wide, powerful back. Damn, everywhere he touched Lawson was hard as rocks and rippled when he moved. The worries about his house and insurance slipped away, as did thoughts about school projects and concerns about the work he had to do and grades. His entire attention centered on the slightly tangy taste of Lawson's lips.

Almost instantly he was as hard as a post, and he leaned into Lawson. That seemed to be a green light because Lawson pulled him closer, pressing his hard chest to Dayne's. God, that was awesome. Soft moans filled the room, and Dayne realized they were his. "Lawson, I…."

"Are you happy?" Lawson whispered, his lips close enough that Dayne felt his breath.

"Yeah." He grinned. Happy, horny, wanting to rub against Lawson the way Tati did when she greeted him because, damn, the man was hot and got his motor running. If Dayne could purr, he'd certainly be doing it.

"Then things are indeed looking up." He kissed Dayne on the lips much more gently this time and then slowly backed away, a prominent bulge in his shorts. "I think I need to go back to my room before things get out of hand." Lawson swallowed and turned away. "I'll see you in the morning."

Dayne watched him go, wishing Lawson was still there, yet pleased as hell at what he'd seen. There had been no mistaking his arousal—that was no small thing. And to think that was the result of him, that Dayne had done that. He lay back on the pillows, turned out the light, put his hands behind his head, and truly smiled for the first time in days.

Chapter 4

LAWSON KNEW no fire was ever routine, but he'd gone in on a sort of autopilot mode, and now he was in some pretty deep shit. He'd been thinking of Dayne, which was no excuse. Dayne had gotten into Lawson's head, and he couldn't get him out. He wished to hell someone had slapped him on the side of the head to pull his attention back to where it should have been.

A neighboring municipality had called for help with a distribution center warehouse that had caught fire. By the time they arrived, the building was still burning, but three workers were unaccounted for. Lawson had volunteered to go inside and look for the man and two women.

He was still searching as chemicals in another part of the facility exploded into an inferno. He dove for the concrete floor, his fire ax sliding out of his hand and across the ground as the heat rolled over him and then upward. He should have paid attention for something like this. Warehouses held all kinds of things, including cleaning supplies and chemicals that could explode. He'd been thinking of Dayne. Now he was alone, separated from Morgan, and might need to be fucking rescued. Shit, he'd made one hell of a mess of this.

"Thank fuck," he mouthed, realizing his breathing apparatus was still functioning. "I'm in the rear of the facility."

No response came over his radio. He was on his own.

The area around him burst into a wall of flame, the contents of the huge racks that filled the place burning heatedly. The bracing began to collapse, littering the aisle behind him. Lawson had seconds before he'd be crushed under the material. He scrambled to his feet and raced forward, then farther back in the warehouse, hoping to get to one of the outside walls and maybe some sort of door. Flashes of flame rolled upward, and Lawson knew he wasn't going to make it. Everything was coming down around him.

A door to the side caught his attention, and he jumped for it and dashed inside as the shelves nearest him collapsed. He slammed the door closed as the ground under his feet shook. Whatever this room was, the shelter wasn't going to last very long.

"What are you doing in here?" he mumbled. The three missing workers lay on the floor. They must have passed out from the fumes and smoke that had filled the room. Even if they were alive, how was he supposed to get them out?

The ground shook again, and fiery debris fell through the ceiling. Lawson raced to the outside wall and found a locked door. Who in the hell locked a fire escape route? There was going to be hell to pay if he got out of this alive. Time was running out. He had to get out and bring these people with him.

A fire extinguisher hung on the wall next to the door. Lawson yanked it down to use it as a battering ram to pound at the lock until it gave way. The rush of fresh air washed over him as Lawson returned, lifted the closest woman, and ran outside. He was at the very back of the facility, with no way to contact the others. He thought little about that and raced back inside. The walls of the room were crumbling around them. Lawson threw the second woman over his shoulder, grabbed the man by the arm and pulled him outside, then slammed the door closed again.

He carried each of the people to the grass and laid them gently on it. Once the last person was clear, the roof over the room they'd been in collapsed, and flames leaped into the air, adding to the column of black smoke that soared toward the sky.

Lawson finally got the attention of one of the other teams, and an ambulance approached through the parking lot of the adjacent warehouse. "Are they alive?" Lawson asked once he could get his gear off and suck in fresh air. Every muscle ached, and he mentally kicked himself for being so reckless. He'd managed to get out and rescue the three missing people, but in the process, he'd nearly died. His heart still pounded a mile a minute. That was one hell of a ride.

"Yes. But the air in that room must have been some kind of toxic stew."

"It was hard as hell to see." The ventilation must have been tied to the rest of the warehouse, and it had likely pumped the fumes inside.

The EMTs administered oxygen, and the two women came around pretty quickly. They sat in the shade with oxygen masks on as the man was loaded into another ambulance for transportation to the hospital.

"What the hell happened to you?" Morgan asked, without the volume of yelling but definitely the intensity. "Your head was somewhere else, and when I turned around, you were fucking gone." His eyes blazed.

"I know. I nearly bought it more than once." It had been sheer luck that he'd found the missing people. "I should have let someone else go in. My head has been...." Even now, as Morgan was giving him hell, part of his feeble brain was dwelling on the kiss he'd shared with Dayne last night. He even grew hard in his fire pants thinking about it.

"What's going on with you?" Morgan hissed low enough that no one else could hear. "Get your head in the game, especially at a fire." He turned toward where the women sat. "It's a damn good thing you found them or your ass would be in a sling."

Lawson's pride refused to allow him to agree vocally, even if he knew Morgan was right. "It looks as though they're going to be okay."

The two women, both short and skinny, one blonde and the other with raven hair, were on their feet as soon as the EMTs took them off the oxygen, and they came over to him. "They said you saved us," the blonde said in a raspy voice, probably from the smoke. "Thank you."

"Yes, thank you. The emergency exit was locked, and we couldn't get out," the other woman said, her voice shaking. "The smoke came in from under the door and through one of the vents, and the fire was outside the interior door. We tried to get out, and then that's all—"

"I understand. I broke the door to get us out." He didn't go into how quickly the walls of the room collapsed or just how close they'd all come to death.

"Did you get Marshall out?"

"Yes. They loaded him into another ambulance. He didn't come around the way you two did."

"He has asthma and breathing problems on a regular basis, so I'm not surprised. He is alive, though?"

"Yes. He was when they took him. I honestly don't know any more than that."

They both nodded. "Well, thank you so much." They smiled a little and returned to where the EMT sat them down to look them over once more.

Lawson gathered his equipment and walked around the still-burning building to where his unit was pouring water on what was left of the structure and its contents.

"I understand you found the missing workers?" Captain Rogers asked.

"Yes. Morgan and I got separated, and I found them in a side office. I got them out. But whoever operated this place had locked the emergency exit door and that's why they couldn't get out."

"I suspect we're going to find a number of violations once we investigate this one." The captain turned to where the other guys were working, and Lawson took that as a dismissal and went over to join them.

He was already worn out. The adrenaline had faded back to normal, and now he was exhausted. Fires got his heart racing, but afterward it was always a letdown, and that was hitting him now.

"Martin, make sure you get checked out when the EMTs are done with the others. You were in there a long time," Captain Rogers said over his shoulder.

Lawson saluted and returned to the EMTs. He let them check him over, and by then there wasn't much of the warehouse left.

"You're good to go. You got scraped up, but that's all."

He knew he'd come so close to much worse. He thanked the EMTs and returned to his unit again, where the guys continued pouring water on the building. "There sure as hell were plenty of combustibles in there."

"What I want to know is why the sprinkler systems didn't switch on," Morgan said, and Captain Rogers nodded.

"Talk to Angus and make sure he knows all the details. He can liaise with the fire marshal's office to make sure they know exactly what we saw. This place was a death trap waiting to happen." Captain Rogers—a twenty-year veteran, graying around the temples and a little overweight—knew fire and how it behaved. "I intend to make these people pay for every violation we can prove."

"We will," Morgan said.

One of the outside walls collapsed inward, and a shower of sparks and flame rose to the sky. They died quickly as water was diverted to the flare-up. Additional units arrived and added more water to the effort, and finally it looked like they were breaking the back of this sucker.

"You two go on home. You've done what you can, and we'll be here for hours mopping this up. I appreciate you both getting in here on your day off." Captain Rogers turned away, and Lawson didn't need to be told twice.

He stripped off the last of his gear and headed back to the station. He stowed his fire gear in his equipment area, cleaned and recharged his breathing apparatus, and put in a requisition for a new fire ax. Then he finally clocked out and drove home.

Dayne wasn't at the house when he got there. If he remembered right, Dayne would either be in class or at the library working on homework or his research projects. He was a hard worker and took his schoolwork seriously. That was something Lawson always had trouble with. He was an action kind of guy, not a classroom or school man.

Lawson got his things into the laundry and then went right upstairs to shower, leaving the door unlocked. He stripped down and was about to start the water when he heard his name drift up the stairs and into the room. He wrapped a towel around his waist and peered out the door. "I'm up here. Is everything okay?"

"That bastard insurance man." Footsteps on the stairs sounded like a charging bull. "He said that there's something suspicious in the fire report, and he wants more information." Dayne reached the top of the stairs, and Lawson realized the second Dayne saw him. He stopped midstride, mouth falling open. "You're naked. I… I… I should just go back downstairs." He said the words, but didn't move.

"Dayne…."

"Yeah." He blinked. "You're way more than cute, you know that?" He didn't turn away. "Oh my God. I'm staring like some idiot and…." He did turn around this time. "I need to shut up and go away."

"Let me finish showering, and I'll come down and you can tell me what's going on. I can have Angus call him personally, and we'll get this straightened out." Lawson had a feeling this was a ploy to try to delay paying. What was wrong with these people? He turned, and the fold holding his towel in place chose that moment to give way.

Dayne squeaked as the towel hit the floor, and Lawson stood there in all his nakedness, his backside on full display. Not that he'd ever been particularly shy, but he was quite afraid poor Dayne would swallow his teeth.

"What happened to the back of your leg and butt?" Dayne asked quietly.

"I got injured in a fire a few years ago." Lawson turned his head to try to look at the scar. He rarely thought of it anymore because it was nearly impossible for him to see unless he twisted just right, and then he could only see part of it. "I was in a house, trying to get the family cat out of an upstairs bedroom, when the hot water heater exploded in the basement. It shot up through the floor, cut the back of my leg and ass, and continued on out of the house through the roof. It was quite spectacular, from what I heard. Of course, I ended up trying to get out of the house with my hands full of angry cat, my leg and ass cut up, and my fire pants ripped to shreds. I'm told half the department saw my ass that day."

"That's one way to get dates," Dayne quipped as Lawson bent to retrieve the towel. "You don't need to do that on my account."

"Well, aren't you cheeky all of a sudden."

Dayne blushed. "You're the one being cheeky, standing there naked, flashing the contest winner for fine butt of the year." It seemed Dayne had a great sense of humor when he let it show.

"I'm about to take a shower." Lawson let the towel dangle in front of him and turned around. "Do you want to join me?" Damn, he loved the way Dayne's eyes bugged out of his head. "You can. I think you'd be beautiful, all wet and slippery."

Dayne squeaked once again. "I...." The heat in his eyes was unmistakable. "Why would someone like you...?" He waved his hands up and down. "I mean, you could be in one of those fireman calendars, and you want me?" Dayne swallowed.

"I was. On a calendar, I mean. They did one two years ago, and I was July."

"Holy shit." Dayne blushed and looked down at himself, then slowly turned away and walked back down the steps.

Lawson swore under his breath. He should have known Dayne would balk. He'd seen the heat and knew Dayne was interested. Hell, he'd vibrated with excitement when Lawson had kissed him. The problem wasn't desire. There was plenty of that on both sides, as evidenced by Dayne's eyes and the fact that Lawson's dick pointed at where Dayne had gone. God, there was something about Dayne that really drew Lawson, and he was used to getting what he wanted. Lawson didn't have trouble capturing guys' attention. They usually came to him. Dayne obviously needed a different approach, and as Lawson went back into the bathroom and turned on the water, he thought he knew what he wanted to do. Dayne was shy and cute, and the things Lawson usually did to get attention were only going to scare him away. The problem was, he wasn't sure how to execute his idea.

"You need to romance him," Richard told him over the phone once Lawson called him after getting out of the shower. "You really like him?"

"You saw him. Dayne is completely adorable, and the way he looks at me is like I hung the moon or something."

"Then don't try to sex him up—romance him. Make him feel as special as he seems to make you feel. Give him the part of yourself you don't show to others."

Lawson swallowed very hard. "I don't do that."

Richard's scoff came through the phone. "You jump out of planes and run into fires to save people. You also free dive off cliffs and would jump off buildings if it wouldn't get you fired, but you're afraid to really open your heart just a little?"

Lawson hummed but didn't give an answer.

"I've known you long enough to know what silence means. You don't want to argue with me. Well, I'm going to tell you this." Richard paused. "Damn it. Give me a second. This chair cushion really bunches." He heard movement and then Richard sighed. "Thanks, Morgan. Where was I? Oh…. If you aren't willing to engage your heart, then you need to leave Dayne alone. He's a nice kid, and he's been through a lot and you know it. Don't add to his misery. If you can't do right by him, just walk away. It'll be easier on both of you."

"Great…."

"I call 'em as I see 'em. Now go on downstairs and take Dayne to dinner or something. Tell him about who you are, and let him see beyond the macho firefighter. If he likes you back, he'll enjoy knowing the real you."

"Okay. Thanks. I really appreciate the advice." Lawson hung up and dialed Angus to explain about the insurance adjuster. Angus said he'd call a contact at the company to find out what was going on. After thanking him, Lawson went downstairs to join Dayne in the living room.

Dayne blushed beet red as soon as he saw Lawson, then hid behind the diary he was reading.

"I didn't mean to make you uncomfortable." Lawson sat in the chair, keeping his distance. "I thought we'd get some dinner together if you like. There's a Japanese restaurant on Carlisle Pike, and we can have sushi."

"I've never tried it, but I like fish." Dayne moved to put the diary aside, but he stopped. "My God. Listen to this."

"December 7, 1908

"He approached me today and we walked in the trees. I'm not sure how much I should write here in case someone finds this book. But I can't keep all this inside. In my tribe, I would not have to fear feeling so for another man. I think Matthew might feel the same. But White men have different names for what I am. Everything is so different here, and Matthew feels the same way I do, so today we walked in the forest and sat under a large tree. My spirit was quiet, so I could listen to the woods and to Matthew. The trees seem to have found their voices again, and I can hear them if I listen. They are just as afraid of the White men as we are sometimes. White men cut all of them down in places and left the land naked.

"It's nice to have a friend. When I'm with the others, I have to be what they want me to be, but with Matthew, I can be myself, and that's wonderful. But the White men are always nearby, watching, so we must be careful.

"Sometimes I feel like my own spirit has deserted me and that I'm turning into a White man. We spend all day learning and speaking English. We read the White man's books and learn the White man's history. But with Matthew, we tell each other our own stories and

59

talk about our villages when the others are not around. He told me he hates it here, but he's doing this because his father wants him to understand the White man so that what's left of his tribe can try to survive. I see the pain in his eyes when he talks about home, and I want to help, but I don't know what to do. I'm trapped here the same way he is.

"They take away everything we know and then try to replace it with what they want us to be. Sometimes I think I'm losing myself, and then I see Matthew and know it's going to be all right. I can talk with him and laugh with him. Matthew makes me happy. I don't know if I can tell him how I feel, so I'm keeping it to myself. It's enough that he's my friend and that I am not alone.

"My warrior inside wishes to rise up, but I cannot, and must do as I'm told."

"Feelings for another man?" Lawson asked. "Does that mean what I think it means?"

"Yes. Today some Native American tribes revere and celebrate the people they call 'two spirits.' In the past it meant they had the spirit of both men and women and they had a special understanding of nature. Not all of them did. It means Ted is saying that he's gay."

"Holy crap." Lawson moved to sit closer. "That's pretty big, and he was taking a huge chance writing that in his journal. What if someone had found it?"

"All I can think is that Ted must have found a good place to hide what he was writing." Dayne closed the diary and held it to his chest, folding his arms over it. "I know exactly how he felt. I was probably the same age when I met the first boy I liked."

"Me too. Robbie Pepperidge," Lawson supplied.

"Jimmy Calhoun." Dayne sighed softly. "I thought he was the living end, and I think he noticed me, but nothing ever came of it. I was too scared and too young to do anything about it. The next year he was dating one of the cheerleaders, and I was still quietly in the closet, still trying to figure things out."

"Robbie and I got further than you did. He was a randy kid, and we used to sneak off together. We arranged to go camping. His folks had a lot of land, and we camped in the woods more than once." Lawson smirked. "I learned a lot about myself and him then."

"What happened?"

"His older brother found us... well, sort of. He came out to check on us, and we had the lights off and had just finished... you know. We heard him and got under the covers, but he scared Robbie so bad that after that, we didn't do anything, and by the end of the summer, Robbie's dad was transferred to New York or something. I never got to see him again. So I understand the rush at Ted's first recognition of someone like him."

"Me too. The way my heart raced and my stomach felt like it was going to flip over and flutter like it had huge butterflies in it. I was both scared and excited at the same time." Dayne gently set the book aside and then sat quietly without saying anything or moving.

"I think we should get some dinner." Lawson got to his feet and waited for Dayne. Tati raced in and jumped onto the sofa. "You be good, and we'll be back soon." Lawson gave her a stroke, and then they left the house and headed to the restaurant.

"Did you get everything done that you wanted to?" Dayne said from the passenger seat as Lawson navigated evening traffic. It began to rain, so he turned on the wipers.

"I got called in. There was a warehouse fire in Mechanicsburg, and they needed help, so I went in with them." He turned on the radio in order to change the subject and provide some quiet background to cover the patter of rain on the windshield. He was just pulling into the restaurant parking lot when the announcer came on.

"We have a local news update. Three workers were rescued from a fire at the Holton Warehouse in Mechanicsburg. One of those rescued is listed in guarded condition, and all others have been released. The warehouse is a total loss, and the investigation is still ongoing."

"Is that the fire you were in?"

"I was the one who got to the last three people."

"Then why didn't you tell me? You're a hero." Dayne smiled over at him as Lawson parked, stopped, and turned off the engine.

"No, I wasn't. Finding them was an accident and luck. I got them out, yeah, but I'm not a hero." Tension flooded into him, and he gripped the wheel tightly before releasing it once again. "Let's go inside and have dinner." He grabbed the umbrella from his door pocket and handed it to Dayne. He got out, raced for the front of the restaurant, and waited for Dayne under the portico.

"You should have waited," Dayne called as he hurried up. "This is big enough for both of us. There's no need for you to get wet."

"It's okay. I didn't want you to get wet." Lawson collapsed the umbrella and shook it off, then held the door for Dayne.

Inside, he asked the hostess for a quiet table, and she led them to a corner of the secondary dining room, placed the menus on the table, and then quietly hurried away.

"This is nice."

"It's family run, and they've been here for quite a while. Some of the best sushi and Japanese food anywhere."

"I've never had sushi, so just order what you think is good, and I'll try it." Dayne simply smiled at him without a hint of worry in his eyes and didn't even open the menu.

Lawson put together a broad selection, hoping Dayne liked it, and asked for water with their dinners. "What sort of things do you do for fun?" he asked once the server had left.

"Well, I like to read, but you probably guessed that already. I can cook, but I'm not very good. Mom was a great cook. She used to make these German meatballs with beef and pork, and she served them in a caper sauce that...." Dayne closed his eyes. "I can still taste them now if I try. I won't be getting them again, though. But it was what Mom made me when I was trying to get back on my feet. I think of it as healing food. What about you?"

"Healing food?" Lawson thought. "Maybe chocolate pudding. When I was growing up and got sick, I'd always lose my appetite and not want to eat. To this day, when I'm sick, I'm never hungry, and

Mom used to try to bribe me with a pudding cup." He smiled. "Even now if I see one, I get a slight bellyache just thinking about it." He leaned closer as they shared a laugh. Dayne's smile was bright, and once his self-consciousness slipped away and he let go of some of his worry, he lit up as if the sun rose behind his head. Such a beautiful, sweet man. "What else do you like to do?"

"I don't know. I used to like to ride horses, but that was a long time ago. I used to help Mom in the garden, but that was more like forced labor. If I was bad, Mom made me weed one of her flowerbeds as punishment."

"I was always cleaning the garage. God, I hated that job. It was always a mess."

"Do you have any brothers or sisters?" Dayne asked.

"I had a sister. But she got sick with leukemia and died when she was twelve. She was something else, even at the end. She never gave up even for a second until she was gone." Lawson drew inspiration from Sheila. She had never complained and always had a smile for him. "That knocked the wind out of my mom for quite a while. She and my dad retired to Ocala, Florida, a few years ago. They sold their house here and figured they'd move and get settled while they were young enough to really enjoy it. So now I'm pretty much alone. I talk to Mom and Dad once or twice a week, but they're off doing their own thing a lot. They take cruises, and my dad works part-time as a systems consultant. He makes enough to pay for what they need, and otherwise, they're off having a grand time."

"You must miss them." The server refilled their waters, and Dayne drank half his glass.

"Of course I do. But they have a good life there. They live in a senior community, and they're always busy with clubs and get-togethers. I'm happy they're happy. Dad worked for years as a computer programmer on mainframe systems and basically became obsolete over the course of his career. It was really hard for him to understand that, and he tried learning new things. But the company wasn't interested in moving him to other things, so when he was able to retire, he started his own business and is doing very well."

"Did your mom work?"

"She taught school, third grade, for years, and I think she was ready to be done when Dad was. Now she tutors kids at a learning center when she wants."

"It sounds ideal for them."

"I like to think so. They're happy." Lawson looked up as the server brought a wooden platform with part of their order neatly laid out on it, and plates for them. "That's pickled ginger and that's wasabi."

"Sounds good." Dayne smiled as he looked over the tray. The server brought a second, and Dayne's mouth hung open a little. "Isn't that a lot?"

"Just try one." Lawson used his chopsticks to cradle one of the smaller pieces and lifted it to Dayne's lips. He took it and chewed, making soft, sexy noises that went right to Lawson's dick. The sounds Dayne made were incredible, and this was only food. Lawson wondered what Dayne would sound like in bed.

"Can I bring you anything else?" the server asked.

"I think we have what we need," Lawson said and smiled. She nodded and left them alone. There was only one other occupied table in the room, and they were in the far corner. It was so intimate at the moment. "Try one of these. It's a dragon roll."

"God...," Dayne said with his mouth full, placing his hand in front of it, but not hiding his grin. "Why haven't I had this before?" He chewed and swallowed. Lawson had been so busy watching Dayne, he almost forgot to eat. "What do you do besides put out fires and rescue people?"

"I garden sometimes. I never thought I'd like it, but once I bought my own house, I wanted it to look nice." Lawson hesitated a little before going on. "I skydive on occasion."

Dayne shook his head. "You're an adrenaline junkie. I can see you doing that." He shivered. "But I can't ever see myself wanting to."

"I like to race boats. I used to have one, and I'd see how fast I could go."

"You mean like the ones you see on those daredevil shows that are always flipping over and flying through the air?" Dayne paused with a bite of sushi halfway to his mouth.

"Yeah. I used to do that. But not anymore. I sold the boat and figured there were better ways of trying to come as close as possible to killing myself without actually doing it." Lawson flashed what he hoped was a disarming smile.

"So now you just run into burning buildings to save people." Dayne's smile was forced. "I...." He set his fork down on the edge of his plate. "I know it's what you do, but I don't understand how you can do that. I'd be too scared, and I'd probably get in there and freeze completely."

"I know it sounds dramatic, but that isn't all I do. A lot of the time I stand by a hose and pour water on buildings to put out the fire. We go in if we believe there could be people trapped inside, and we only do it if we believe it's possible for us to come out again."

"Yeah, but a lot can happen."

"Yes, it can." There was no arguing with that after the near miss he'd had earlier. "I have a lot of special equipment for breathing, communication, as well as just to protect my body. I'll show it to you sometime."

"Is it really heavy?"

"It can be, but we have to carry what we need with us when we go into a building like that. We practice and train a lot for all situations. But sometimes reality throws us a curve, and we need to be ready for those too. I'm a good fireman, and I love what I do."

Dayne reached across the table and curled his hand around two of Lawson's fingers. "I understand that. But it's frightening for me. I keep losing people in my life, so it's a little hard to see you... well, taking chances with yours." He took another drink of water. "I know it's what you do, but it seems dangerous... and, I suppose, very exciting."

"It can be." Lawson took another sushi roll and ate it, using the time to get his thoughts together. He leaned over the table. "Imagine you arrive on the scene of a home on fire, with flames poking out of the front window, and a mother races up to the truck, saying her child is in there. We assess the situation, and I'm already getting my breathing equipment on. By the time the captain makes his decision, I'm ready, and he gives the word. One of the other guys is ready, too, with a hose, and we break down the door and race inside.

"There's fire lapping up the walls, but the mother said the girl is upstairs. Every second counts, because the more the fire burns, the less stable the house gets. The hose guy with me is already pouring water on the place, and I take the stairs as fast as I can. There's smoke and flames around me, and it's hard to see. I push open doors and, of course, the last one is a little girl's room. But she isn't in there. I look around and find her huddled under the bed."

Dayne appeared to hang on each word, clearly caught up in the story.

"She's terrified, but I help her out, grab a blanket to throw over her, and head back the way I came. As we reach the top of the stairs, the hose man sprays down the area ahead of us, and I hurry down and race for the front door as the man with the hose follows us out."

Dayne sat back, drinking more water, his eyes wide. "My heart is pounding and that was just a story."

"Imagine how it feels to actually be there. That's part of what I do. The mother is overjoyed to see her daughter, and they hug when I place her in her mom's arms. There's nothing better than the look of relief and happiness on the mother's face." Lawson grinned because he just couldn't help it. He'd seen the looks on parents', wives', husbands', and even children's faces when he brought out their loved ones to them.

"What happens if…?"

"I don't get there in time?" Lawson sighed and set down his chopsticks. "It happens, and it hurts every time. I've held mothers and fathers back as they screamed to get inside a house that was collapsing in front of them." It damn near broke his heart each time, but that was part of the job. Rescue those they could and keep others from getting hurt.

"Is that what you like most about your job? Rescuing people?" Dayne slowly ate another bite.

"The thing I like best is when I get to go to schools and talk to the kids about fire safety. They're so excited, and their eyes light up when I get there. I show them my equipment and get to demonstrate how I help people. I also teach them how they can be safer in their own homes." He snagged another piece of sushi.

"I think I'd like to see that sometime. I bet you're amazing with kids."

"They're so much fun, and they have so much energy. If we can, we arrange for a truck to stop by so they can see one up close." Lawson sat back, stuffed to the gills. Dayne was still eating, and he watched. Each movement was so graceful and flowing. Whenever Dayne parted his lips for a bite, Lawson wanted to lean over the table to kiss him.

"This was an amazing dinner." Dayne set his fork down and leaned back in his chair. "Thank you." He fidgeted slightly, wiggling in his seat. "You've been so good to me... too good, and I can't continue to take advantage of you."

"You aren't. Believe me. The house is big enough, and...." He didn't want Dayne to leave.

"I'll call the adjuster tomorrow. The stalling is driving me crazy. The fire was an accident, and they know it. They have to have an answer on my claim very soon, and then I can start work rebuilding the house. I know it's going to take time, and I'm going to need to find a place to live until then. I've put some feelers out near the college and will see what comes up."

"Then take what time you need. But don't worry about it." Lawson reached into his pocket, pulled out a key ring, and handed it to Dayne. "I have to go back on regular shifts tomorrow, so I'm not going to be home nearly as much for the next week or so. This way you can get in when you need to." Lawson had no idea why the thought of Dayne leaving caused him so much worry.

"You must be busy…. You don't need me hanging around all the time."

The truth was, other than work and some of his buddies there, Lawson lived a pretty lonely life. "A lot of my friends have married or paired off over the years, and I see them, but not as much as I used to. They have family things that they do now."

Dayne leaned forward. "So you're saying you're lonely too."

"Yeah, I guess I am. I work a lot of hours, and there isn't a lot of time for me to go out and make friends. I've gone to the clubs sometimes, but that's generally to meet people for a very different purpose, and most of the time names aren't really top of the priority, let alone anything else other than…." Lawson liked his life. Well, he thought he did. But his life was work, more work, and then downtime at home where he mostly thought about work and prepared for going back to work. "I like having you at my house, and you can stay there as long as you like. I didn't mean to make you uncomfortable earlier." God, if this was about his stunt with the towel, he was going to kick himself like there was no tomorrow.

"You didn't." Dayne lowered his voice. "It's just that no one has been interested in me in a long time. I'm not exactly a catch. Richard has some friends, and one of them is the owner of Bronco's downtown. Morgan and Richard took me there once to meet people, but I felt like a complete freak. A few guys talked to me, but as soon as they saw how I walked, they couldn't get away fast enough."

Lawson's hands clenched into fists. Somehow he managed not to bang the table. "I'm sorry." People could be so cruel. The server brought the check, and Lawson handed her his credit card and signed the slip when she returned. "Shall we?"

They huddled under the umbrella and made for the car. Lawson started the engine and got the air moving to push away the mustiness as they pulled out of the lot. He turned and continued past where he'd normally turn to go home.

"Where are we going?"

"To have a little fun. I think you deserve it." Lawson gently patted Dayne's thigh and continued east, crossing the bridge into Harrisburg. He parked on Third Street, thanks to his emergency vehicle plates. The rain had slowed to a drizzle, and he opened Dayne's door and let him out before guiding him toward the club.

"You're taking me to Bronco's?" Dayne sounded more than a little skeptical.

"Yup. We're going to dance."

Dayne chuckled nervously. "I don't dance. My legs don't move that way."

Lawson put an arm around Dayne's shoulders and leaned in very close. "I bet you dance wonderfully, and I want to show you." He paid the cover at the door, and they went inside.

The music pulsed and throbbed, getting right to Lawson's spine, the energy intoxicating. He'd forgotten how much he loved this place. Dayne tensed next to him, and Lawson held his hand tightly, letting Dayne know he wasn't going to let go.

"Hey, I haven't seen you in here in a while." A guy Lawson had let suck him off in the bathroom once sauntered over, swaying his skinny hips to the beat of the music. "You want to dance?"

"Go on and have fun." Dayne pulled his hand away and was already heading toward the door. Lawson turned without a word and gently slid an arm around Dayne's waist.

"I plan to have fun… with you." Lawson touched Dayne's chin. "I brought you here so we could have fun together." He guided Dayne toward the floor, parting people as he went. When he found a good spot, he held Dayne's hands and moved to the music, simply, slowly, until Dayne mimicked him. "That's it."

"But people are watching."

Lawson lowered Dayne's hands, sliding them around his waist. "Let them watch. They're just jealous because I already have you and they can't." He pulled Dayne to him, and they moved together.

Let anyone who wanted to look, look. Dayne was his, and he wasn't going to let him go.

The song ended, and the music shifted to something slower. Lawson ran his hands down Dayne's back, cradling him, smiling for all the world when Dayne relaxed and put his head on his chest. He leaned forward, sniffing Dayne's hair and letting everyone else in the place recede. He had what he really wanted.

"Excuse me," some kid said as he danced up, pressing right to Lawson's side. "I'm Colt, and you can ride me like the stallion you are."

Dayne snickered and lifted his head. "Does a line like that really work? Because it's lame as hell. See if it works on someone else, because this particular stallion is mine, and I'll claw your eyes out if you try again. Spread the word."

"No need to have a hissy fit." Colt danced off in search of some other horse he could ride, and Dayne returned his head to where it had been.

"Stupid twink," Dayne growled, and Lawson smiled.

"I like it when you stand up for yourself." They continued dancing. "It's sexy, and don't argue with me on this. It is, and so are you." Lawson held Dayne a little tighter, and when the music changed, becoming faster and more frenetic, he guided him off the floor toward the bar, where a huge man stood with his arms over his chest... watching.

"That's Bull," Dayne told him. "He's part owner of the club and the friend of a friend, I guess you could say. He helped me the last time I was here."

The large, bald-headed man made his way over. "You're a friend of Richard and Morgan's."

"Yeah. Dayne, and this is Lawson. He works with Morgan and Angus." They both shook hands with Bull.

"I haven't seen you here recently, Dayne. I hope you're both having a good time." Bull never seemed to stop scanning the club.

"We are." Dayne turned, and the gentle look on his face was enough to outshine the sun. "Lawson brought me here to dance."

"Well, you both have a good time." Bull became agitated and then hurried off around the edge of the crowd. Dayne leaned closer to Lawson and looked toward the bar.

"I'll get us something to drink," Lawson offered and pointed to a table that was empty. Another couple was making their way over to it, and Lawson stepped between them to give Dayne a chance to sit. "I'll be right back." He gave Dayne a soft kiss and then hurried to the bar.

It was packed with people, and Lawson waited his turn. A number of guys approached him, trying to get his attention. He was polite but didn't show any interest, and they went about their business. He was with Dayne, and that was more than enough. The attention they offered was not at all what Lawson was interested in. He got a couple of beers and some bottles of water, and returned to where Dayne waited, rubbing his legs.

Lawson set the glasses on the table. "Are you okay? Do your legs hurt? We can go if you want to. I just wanted to give you some better memories than the ones you'd had before."

Dayne took one of the beers and drank most of it in a few gulps. "God, that's good, and my leg is fine. Sometimes I rub them just because I'm used to them aching and half expect them to begin hurting. It's become so normal… too normal, I guess." Dayne swayed to the music as they sat and finished their drinks.

"Do you want to dance some more?"

"If they play a few slower songs."

The guys on the floor bounced and writhed to the pulsingly fast beat. Lawson was afraid it was too fast for Dayne to move to. He'd found that instead of moving his feet, Dayne simply swayed to the music and let Lawson do the rest.

"They will." Lawson winked and downed the last of his beer before opening the water. He drank and dang near emptied the bottle. The club was kept a bit warm to encourage people to drink, and it worked exceedingly well. He finished his water, and just as Dayne was doing the same, the music changed. Lawson took Dayne's hand, led them back to the dance floor, and held him as they swayed back and forth.

He loved having Dayne in his arms. It was a magical experience, and every time Dayne lifted his gaze, the smile on his lips was more than worth anything in the world. Dayne was happy, and that was enough to power the world—well, at least Lawson's world.

After a couple of songs, the music changed once again, so they headed for the door. There was no use sticking around. They had done what they came here to do, and Lawson could tell that Dayne's legs were starting to bother him. He didn't want Dayne hurting. In fact, just the opposite. "Are you ready to go?"

"I should use the bathroom." Dayne turned, then shook his head and continued toward the door. "I'll wait till we get home." He leaned on Lawson, holding his arm as they walked.

"What's this, cripple's day out?"

The words reached Lawson's ears, and he knew where they had come from. But taking care of the asshole would mean leaving Dayne, and he wasn't going to do that.

They stepped outside, and Lawson nodded to the bouncer and turned, and they continued down the street to his car.

"Give me your wallets," a guy said from behind them.

Lawson had been on alert because of the earlier comment. He released Dayne, whipped around, and knocked the man's feet out from under him. The man went down hard, and the knife he'd been carrying flew from his hand and skittered along the sidewalk.

Lawson pressed his keys into Dayne's hand. "Get in the car and lock the door." He was ready in case the guy got up, but the guy just groaned and rolled on the ground. Lawson called the police as a pair of bouncers from the club hurried up to them.

"I saw what happened. Are you both all right?"

"Yes. He tried to rob us and got a lot more than he bargained for." Lawson wasn't going to take crap from a low-life mugger, and certainly not when Dayne could have gotten hurt. "The police are on their way."

"Where's your friend?" the huge, intimidating bouncer asked.

"He's in the car. I wanted to make sure he was safe in case Mr. Brilliant here tried anything more."

Lawson waited until the police arrived, then explained what happened. An ambulance was called, and Lawson gave a statement. The police also talked to Dayne, and then they were allowed to go. Lawson got in the car, started the engine, and headed for home a lot later than he'd intended.

"Do you have class tomorrow?"

"No. It's Saturday and I'm off. I thought I'd work on my projects. I can go to the library if you don't want me at the house all day when you're not there. I'm also hoping it's okay to call Angus to see what the insurance people told him. This whole thing with them is starting to sound like something I'm going to need a lawyer for." He sighed heavily.

"I don't mind you being at the house. And Angus is really good at getting people to do what needs to be done. Call him in the morning, but not too early. I don't know if he's on shift, but I'll give you his cell number and you can try him there. He was pretty angry when I talked to him."

"That's good. The more people on my side, the better."

They reached the house, and Lawson let them inside. He went right to the basement to get his bag packed and ready for the morning. When he finished, Lawson left it at the base of the stairs and joined Dayne in the living room.

"Go on up to bed if you like. I need to feed Tati, and I'll set out a container of food for her."

"Okay." Dayne pulled his feet under him, and Tati settled on his lap. It really did look as though Lawson's cat had found a new favorite person. Dayne got out one of his books and quietly read as Lawson finished what he needed to do.

Dayne was still reading when Lawson locked the doors and went upstairs. He turned at the top of the steps as the lights downstairs switched off, and Dayne followed him up. Lawson waited for him, took his hand, and kissed Dayne good night before going to his room.

He had decided it was best to wait and let Dayne tell him when he was ready to move forward. Each day it got harder, because every night, Lawson dreamed of Dayne in vivid detail. The waiting was giving him a massive case of blue balls, but Dayne deserved to be treated as though he were special, and Lawson was determined to be patient.

He used the bathroom first and came out, passing Dayne in the hallway.

"Do you always do that?" Dayne motioned to the fact that Lawson was in only a pair of sleep shorts.

"What?"

"Run around the house nearly naked when you have others over."

"Nope." Lawson stepped closer. "I only do it when someone is here who I want to notice me."

He turned, went back to his room, and closed the door. He climbed into bed and rolled over, closing his eyes. Lawson knew Dayne was attracted to him, and he cared for Dayne, enough that he was going to let Dayne determine the speed at which things went between them. He wasn't going to push or make the first move, any more than he already had. From here on out, it was up to Dayne to figure out what he wanted.

Lawson only hoped he could be patient enough that Dayne would eventually come to him.

Chapter 5

DAYNE LAY in bed, almost afraid to move. Tati had come in a few minutes earlier and pressed up against him after kneading the covers to her satisfaction. The house was quiet, but Dayne's mind was anything but. He kept seeing Lawson in nothing but those shorts, and he wondered what it would be like to have Lawson holding him like he had on the dance floor, only with a lot less clothes.

Dayne rolled over and groaned. Why the hell was he being such a huge chicken? It wasn't like he hadn't had sex before. He just hadn't since the accident, and what if Lawson saw his legs and freaked out? They weren't pretty, and if Lawson thought he was ugly, then forget about the hope that was currently running rampant inside him.

He wondered what would happen if he got out of bed and went to Lawson's room. He was pretty sure Lawson wanted him to, but what if he was reading everything wrong and made a fool of himself? Yeah, Lawson had taken him dancing and held him close, but that could be because he was being nice. "What do you think, Tati?"

Oh crap. He was asking advice from Lawson's cat. His cheese really was getting ready to fall off the cracker.

Dayne came to the conclusion that he could lie here all night and wonder, or just get up and see what the possibilities were. But, damn it, he was scared. Lawson had been so nice to him, but that didn't mean he was interested in him in that way. God, Dayne wished he'd asked outright. Lawson had said he was sexy and he'd put on that show earlier, but what if he was teasing?

"Jesus Christ." His legs were damaged in the accident, not his backbone, and maybe he needed to find it. Dayne got out of bed, leaving Tati in her nest, and quietly left the room. He stopped and turned, looking toward Lawson's door. Dayne quietly walked down to it and tried to look inside, but he saw nothing. Slowly he pushed the door open and peered around it.

"Dayne?" Lawson asked, and he stopped. "Is something wrong?"

"No. I was wondering if…." He paused, thinking he should just go back to his room.

Lawson didn't move at first, but then slowly lifted the covers and slid over on the mattress. He didn't say anything; if he had, Dayne might have run. His heart beat so fast, he could hear it in his ears, and it was more than a little disconcerting and thrilling at the same time. He took a step into the room as Lawson held his hand still, clearly issuing an invitation, one Dayne wanted to accept so very badly.

He approached the bed and lay down.

Lawson lowered the soft sheet over him and tugged him close. "It's all right. Nothing is going to happen that you don't want." Lawson kissed his shoulder, snaking his hand around Dayne's belly, pressing his chest to Dayne's back. "There you are. Just relax."

That was so much easier said than done, with Lawson's long, thick cock pressed to his butt. Damn, he'd seen hints, but the man was big. Dayne wasn't sure what he wanted to happen tonight. Did he want to have sex with Lawson? Yeah. Did he want Lawson to use his mouth on him? He quivered a little at the thought.

"There's nothing to be worried about." Lawson must have taken his shiver for fear instead of excitement. "Like I said, just relax and close your eyes. It's been a very long day for both of us, and we need our rest."

"But…."

"This is enough for now. Having you here with me is wonderful." Lawson gently rubbed small circles on his belly but made no move to initiate anything more.

"I thought you were interested in me."

"I am, sweetheart. More than just interested. But taking time isn't an indication of disinterest. It means I care enough and want you enough to wait." Lawson shifted away, and Dayne lay on his back. "You're worth the wait."

Dayne swallowed hard. "No one's said I was worth anything in so long that...."

"Then they're fools." Lawson lay next to him, an arm over his chest, sending heat right to the center of him.

Dayne wondered what he'd done to get this lucky. He lifted Lawson's arm, brought his hand to his mouth, and kissed Lawson's fingers. That was so nice to hear. Dayne wanted to believe it, but it was going to take time.

"I know people have treated you badly and that you've been hurt. I don't want to do that, and I'll do my best to let you know how I feel."

"But the bad stuff is so much easier to believe." Dayne closed his eyes. There had been so much over the last few years. He knew he was damn lucky to have found Lawson. It was still hard for him to believe someone as hot as Lawson would look at him with anything but pity. This whole idea was going to take some getting used to, and he was going to need time to try to build up the trust Lawson was implicitly asking for.

Dayne rolled over to face Lawson, and was gently guided into a kiss that he felt all the way to his toes. He wanted more and scooted closer, Lawson's legs parting his, their hips pressing together.

"Sweetheart, I know things are moving fast, but we need to take things more slowly. Make sure you understand what you want. I'm not going anywhere." Lawson yawned.

"Oh, I guess you're tired."

"I have to be up quite early in the morning. Usually between shifts I stay at the station, but I'll be home tomorrow evening, and then I'll go back for my shift."

"But don't you need to be on call?"

"Yes, and I may have to leave at a moment's notice, but I'd rather spend a few hours with you." Lawson held him close, and they settled quietly. The energy between them was still there, only instead of sizzling, it was banked, burning low. Dayne once again lay on his back, closing his eyes as he listened to Lawson breathe.

He tried to remember the last time he'd slept with someone just to sleep, and couldn't. It had to have been with Jeff. They'd spent many nights together, and not all of them were for sex. Jeff had been a very special man, and Dayne held back the flood of memories he'd tried to keep in a box, but it was breaking open, as were a number of things in his life.

"What are you thinking about?"

Dayne hesitated. "I'm trying to remember the last time I felt like this."

"With Jeff?"

"Yeah. He was ripped away from me so quickly. It wasn't fair. Jeff didn't deserve to die. Neither of us had done anything to deserve this kind of pain, and though I keep trying to find a reason for it, there isn't one. I know that now. Bad shit happens, and what scares me is that I keep expecting it now. Whenever something good happens to me, I brace for what's coming, because there's always a price to pay. Jeff and I were happy and talking about getting married, and *wham*! I was just getting my life together again when I lost Mom. *Wham*! Then I get this great opportunity at school, but my house burns down. *Wham! Wham!*"

Lawson stroked his belly. "Maybe you're looking at things a little backward. See, your house burning down had nothing to do with you doing well at school. But your house burning down did put me across your path once again, so maybe the bad thing was losing the house, and the good thing was that I got to meet and get to know you. It wasn't likely we'd cross paths otherwise, and not meeting you would have been a real shame." Lawson quieted, and Dayne didn't argue with him. Maybe there was a bright side to this after all.

Just as Dayne was about to fall asleep, he heard a *humph* as Her Highness jumped onto the bed and made herself comfortable near Dayne's legs. This was nice, and if he let himself, Dayne could see this becoming something he really could get used to.

THE FOLLOWING morning when Dayne woke, sun streamed through the windows and he was alone, except for a cat lying on his chest, blinking down at him. She butted his head, turned, and jumped off the bed in her attempt to say it was feeding time. "All right."

Dayne pushed back the covers and got out of bed. His legs ached as soon as he put his feet on the floor. God, this was a regular thing. Nights meant his legs stayed still much of the time, so they stiffened up, and it could take a while for him to loosen the muscles. Tati was impatient and hurried to the door and then back. Dayne went to his room, pulled on a T-shirt, and then went down the stairs with the cat racing ahead of him.

He found a note in the kitchen explaining what Tati should be fed.

I slept like a baby last night, and that was because you were there. Holding you was special, and I look forward to doing it again tonight.

It was signed Lawson, with a smiley face. Dayne read the note again until Her Highness decided he'd taken long enough. He fed her and then went back upstairs to get cleaned up and dressed.

He found some bread and made toast for breakfast before sitting in the living room. He turned on the television to a local station for some news and promptly ignored it as he pulled out his books. Tati joined him on the sofa and curled next to him.

When he got into his work, school or otherwise, even as a kid, his mother used to say the house could fall down around him and he wouldn't notice. That was still true, and only his rumbling stomach pulled him away from his outline for his thesis, well into the afternoon. He glanced at the television and hit Mute. Figuring he could walk to one of the cafés a few blocks away, he got up. He thought the movement would do him good, but his legs told him otherwise, so Dayne ended up driving through a fast-food place and then returning to the house to eat his chicken nuggets. He even shared one of them with Tati, who seemed to have a real appetite for chicken. Then he figured he could take a break and gave Angus a call.

"This is Dayne. Lawson said it was okay to call you."

"Yes… I spoke with the representative from the insurance company and told him exactly what we found and reiterated what was in the report. He seemed skeptical, so I pulled out the big guns. I told him that unless he was willing to take on the entire fire department and could prove the report was inaccurate, which he can't, that he needed to move ahead, or I'd have the department file a grievance with the insurance commission."

Dayne smiled. "What did he say?"

"They hear threats like that all the time. So I asked him if he knew who Joe Martinelli—the head of the commission—was. Of course he did, and I said that I could call him right now, and asked for his number so Joe could call him back. I think the claim is going to move forward."

"Do you really know that guy?"

"Yeah. He used to be a neighbor growing up, and I know they're going after companies who jerk around their policyholders. It was a huge issue in the last gubernatorial campaign, so the state is being vigilant at the moment. And I suggest that once this is settled, you find another company. Make them pay out and then drop them."

"That was the plan. Thank you. Being here with Lawson is nice, but I need to get my life back together, and I can't take Lawson's hospitality for granted."

"You're very welcome." Angus ended the call, and Dayne returned to his work.

The classes at Dickinson required more work than most of his classes at Penn State. But he was loving his studies, and each class was a challenge. He'd always been good in school, and he and Jeff had had so many plans for what they wanted to do together. All that changed for so many years while he was healing, both from his injuries and from the loss of the man he thought of as the love of his life.

Dayne pulled his thoughts away from those topics and back to the work at hand. He had a paper due in the middle of next week for his American studies class, so he got busy on that, settling his computer on his lap as he dove into the cultural significance of the romance novel. Dinner snuck up on him the same way lunch had, and he found the makings for a sandwich and went back to work until a story on the evening news caught his attention.

It was a building fire, with footage of flames shooting into the trees surrounding the building. Dayne turned on the sound. "The house is still burning out of control. We're told that firefighters have gotten the family out and are now concentrating on putting out the fire. One firefighter was injured and has been taken to a local hospital for treatment."

The news show moved on, and Dayne texted Lawson. He went back to work but wasn't getting very far, waiting for Lawson's response.

I'm fine. We weren't called to that fire. CU in a few hours.

Dayne released the breath he'd been holding since he saw the story and only then realized how worked up he'd gotten over it. Lawson was okay, and Dayne turned off the television and set his schoolwork aside. He was ahead now, and had even caught up on his reading. So he found a movie, lay on the sofa, with Tati crawling onto his belly, and settled in to wait for Lawson to come home.

"HEY." LAWSON leaned over the sofa as Dayne opened his eyes. "You must have been tired."

"Sorry. I meant to wait up for you. Did you have a lot of calls?"

"A few. Mostly general emergency calls and one kitchen grease fire." Lawson yawned, and Dayne sat up to give him room on the sofa.

"Are you hungry? I can make you a sandwich or something." Dayne rubbed his eyes and hurried to the kitchen without waiting for an answer. "Do you like grilled cheese? I can make one for you. I saw slices in the fridge." Dayne was already getting the stuff out when Lawson joined him in the kitchen. "Just tell me where the pans are."

"You don't need to do this. I can have some crackers or something."

Dayne found the frying pans and set to making the sandwiches. "I saw the fire on television, and I was worried about you. They said they took a firefighter to the hospital. Did you know who it was?"

"Yeah. Angus was on that call, and he got too much smoke. He was taken as a precaution, and he's home with Kevin now. Sometimes the news makes more of things than necessary because they have fifteen seconds to get the story out and move on to the next one." Lawson sat on one of the stools, elbows on the counter, resting his head on his hands. He looked super tired and about ready to fall over. Dayne put a sandwich on and got plates and some glasses, then poured Lawson a glass of grape juice from the bottle in the fridge.

"I'd rather have a beer."

"You're already tired, and something to replace the energy you've lost will help." Dayne also took out a can of beer, and Lawson drank the juice in two gulps. Dayne passed him a sandwich and began making another. He figured Lawson would have a healthy appetite once he got some food in him.

"What did you do today?"

"I got a paper nearly written and did some of the exercises that were assigned."

"Is this the paper on the Indian School?"

"No. It's for another class. I'm just getting my materials together for that paper, and it will take a few more weeks of research before I really need to start writing it." He hadn't had a chance to look at it again since he'd been working to catch up on everything else.

Lawson had finished inhaling his sandwich, and Dayne put the second one on his plate before making one for himself.

"I thought I'd get to it tomorrow while you were at work." He leaned over the counter. "I wanted to spend what time you had available with you since you were coming home instead of staying at the station."

"Thanks." Lawson tugged him closer. "I kept thinking of you all day. Every time I had a chore to finish, I wondered what you were doing." He rolled his eyes. "I think I'm turning into a teenage girl."

"Why, because you have feelings and are showing them?" Dayne smacked Lawson lightly on the shoulder. "You aren't really one of those guys who grunts, burps, and farts and calls it communication. Having feelings isn't a bad thing, and letting me see them is hot."

"Hot?"

"Yeah. I think it's hot if a guy can be vulnerable. But then, you're talking to the guy who cried like a baby on your shoulder the night his house burned down, so maybe I'm not the best judge of emotional stability."

"You handled it just fine, and if you must know, I don't talk about my feelings. I tend to act on them."

Dayne rolled his eyes. "So you do stupid shit and then make people wonder why?" He was having fun with this. "It's easier to talk about stuff."

"Maybe for you. I'm an action kind of guy. If I'm upset, I go to the guy who bothered me. If I'm pissed off, I call up some friends and arrange to jump out of an airplane."

"I forgot you said you jumped out of planes."

"When I went out West on vacation a few years ago, I did some BASE jumping. That was awesome as well. I haven't been hang gliding, but I'd like to try that next."

Dayne stared openmouthed. "Do you have some kind of death wish?"

"No. I like excitement. It's part of why I became a firefighter. But what I didn't understand about the job at the time was that it was hours of waiting around for a few minutes of doing something interesting. I still love it, though."

Dayne picked up half of his sandwich and took a bite. He felt himself pulling back into his shell like a startled turtle. Lawson did all those daring things, and Dayne.... This whole thing between them was a pipe dream. It had to be. There was no way Dayne could ever do any of that, and it was just a matter of time before Lawson got tired of him and decided he wanted someone he *could* do all those daring things with. He swallowed, but the cheese tasted flat, and the bread hung in his mouth. Suddenly he wasn't hungry anymore and passed his uneaten half of sandwich to Lawson, who finished it off.

Dayne took care of the dirty plates and finished his juice before leaving the room. He gathered his school things, then said good night to Lawson and went up the stairs. He figured he might as well back away and make a break between them before he got too far down a road that was only going to lead to disappointment. He brushed his teeth and went to his room, then closed the door and climbed into bed. He wanted to burrow in somewhere and hide. He'd let himself think... dream... that maybe someone like Lawson could find him interesting. But there was no way. Dayne could never keep up with him or be part of the excitement Lawson so obviously craved.

He pulled the diary out of his pack, needing something to take his mind off his misery. He read a few entries about daily activities and sports. Then everything changed.

January 9, 1909
He kissed me. Today Matthew kissed me, and I kissed him back. It snowed last night and we needed more wood for the stove, so

Matthew and I volunteered to get more. We were behind the woodpile. I had an armload of wood. Matthew stared into my eyes, and I couldn't move. His eyes were deep brown and swirled with something I didn't recognize. Then he leaned in and kissed me.

I dropped the wood on his foot, and he hopped around on one leg but said nothing. I felt really bad and returned his kiss as soon as he stopped jumping. I think his pain was forgotten after that. I hope so.

Dayne smiled, laying the diary on his chest as he thought of the headiness of a first kiss.

We parted and filled our arms with wood to take back to the dormitory, my steps light. I tried not to look at him differently, because two boys kissing would not be tolerated here. I'd already seen the White man's justice with people like me… and Matthew. And I don't want anything to happen to either of us.

Dayne shivered as he thought of the consequences of someone at the school reading what he had just read. Ted was taking a real chance writing down his thoughts like this.

There was a large blank space on the page.

I found a secure hiding place for this so no one will know about Matthew and me. I'm not going to write down where it is, but my thoughts will truly be safe now.

I am still a warrior.

Dayne blinked as tears welled in his eyes. To think that in a place like that, so far away from what they both knew, Ted and Matthew had been able to find happiness of some sort. At least that's what Dayne wanted to think. They'd kissed, and he could imagine the feelings blooming inside both of them: recognition, care, maybe even the beginnings of love. He wanted to read more to find out what happened, but a soft knock on the door pulled his thoughts away. "Yes."

Lawson opened the door and put his head in. "What's wrong?"

Dayne sighed and set the diary on the bedside table, blinking away the tears that threatened. "Just reading and thinking." He sat up slowly. "I should move to a hotel tomorrow and get out of your hair."

Lawson came inside. "Why?"

"You do all those daring, active things that you love, but I can't do any of them, and I never will. What will happen when you realize I'm just an anchor around your neck? The thought of jumping out of a plane is enough to nearly make me wet myself, and even if it didn't scare me to death, I could never do it with my legs." Dayne turned away. He had to look somewhere else or Lawson was going to see his pain, and he didn't want that.

"Those are things I do for fun. I also garden and read. I like movies, and—"

"But can you tell me you're not going to get tired of me? I know I would if I was into all that cool stuff. Hell, Lawson, you jump off cliffs, and I couldn't even walk to the top so I could jump off."

"Do you think those things are what's really important? I like the thrill sometimes."

Dayne sighed. "But I can't be part of that. You do realize that I saw that story on the news and worried that you might have gotten hurt. It was just a news story, and I was already too worried to work until I heard from you. That's your job, and I could live with that. But I'd be scared half to death if I knew you were jumping out of an airplane or off the tops of cliffs." Lawson sat on the edge of the bed, and Dayne wiped his eyes before turning back around. "You deserve a whole man who can do the things you like with you. Not someone like me who'll just sit home and worry while you're out having fun."

Lawson put his hand on his shoulder. "Have you ever thought that maybe I was doing all those things because I didn't have someone thrilling and special here at home?"

Dayne rolled his eyes. "Come on. You want me to believe that all that stuff you talked about was because you were lonely and just looking for the geek of your dreams?"

"I was lonely, yes, and I don't know about the geek part." Lawson smiled. "Dayne, you don't need to worry so much about what you can't do. Be happy with the things you can. I don't expect you to skydive or jump off cliffs with me, and I doubt the BASE jumping is something I'm going to make a habit of. As for the skydiving, I have friends with a plane and I go up with them every few months."

"But you're used to exciting things, and I'm anything but."

"I don't know about that." Lawson bumped his shoulder and then leaned closer, sniffing the base of his neck before lightly kissing it. God, that felt so damn good. Dayne's resolve slipped away. He wanted to think Lawson would be interested in him, because dang it all, he wanted Lawson so badly he could taste it. Lawson was a good guy and he really did seem to like Dayne. That was what hurt the most. Lawson probably did like him. Dayne tried not to think of how he was going to feel when Lawson realized Dayne wasn't the kind of guy he needed.

Dayne turned, and Lawson kissed him, sliding a hand through his hair to cup his head. Dayne closed his eyes and moaned softly. This was too good to just walk away from. His mind said this was a recipe for disaster, but his heart wanted Lawson so much it felt like it was going to explode. Dayne knew he should stop, should put an end to this, but Lawson pressed him back on the bed, and Dayne wound his arms around his neck, deepening the kiss. When Lawson broke the kiss, the haze cleared from Dayne's mind and he pulled away.

"Leave your hands there," Lawson said firmly, and Dayne did as he said. Lawson slid his arms under him, lifted him off the bed, and carried him down to Lawson's bedroom. He laid him on the bed, leaned close, and licked and then sucked at one of Dayne's nipples until Dayne groaned and lay back on the bed, the last of his resistance crumbling under a tidal wave of heat.

87

"Lawson, we…." Dayne gasped.

"Are you saying we shouldn't do this?" Lawson asked huskily, his voice deep and gravelly.

"But what if you don't want me later?" Dayne didn't want to know the answer to that.

Lawson sucked and kissed his way down Dayne's belly to his sleep pants, sending ripples racing through him. When Lawson reached for the waistband, Dayne closed his eyes and let Lawson lower them over his hips and then down his scarred legs. He held still, waiting for the gasp and the revulsion he was certain was just seconds away. Dayne tried not to think about the humiliation that was coming.

Lawson stroked his legs, his touch gentle. When Dayne opened his eyes, he expected to see a grimace, but Lawson looked back at him with such care. "I knew you went through a lot, but…." Lawson bounded up to him and kissed him hard. "You have more strength than—" Lawson kissed him again, cutting off his own words.

"But my legs." Dayne pushed at Lawson's shoulders. "You saw what they look like."

"And they're part of you and part of what you've been through. The scars are certainly nothing to be ashamed of. They're war wounds, and you survived."

Dayne shook his head on the pillow. "I was never in the war." The excitement had died, and he was starting to feel self-conscious, lying naked on the bed.

"Yes, you were. You went through hell and came out of it on top." Lawson ran his hands down Dayne's legs as though they were normal.

"I came out of it a mess and barely able to walk."

Lawson stopped, his hands resting on Dayne's thighs. "Your legs are part of you." Lawson stoked gently upward, along his inner thighs, then lightly cupped his balls. *God.* Dayne closed his eyes again, trying not to let his fear override the pleasure. "Just like anything else.

The accident became part of you and helped make you the caring, gentle man you are."

"Boring…," Dayne corrected.

"Sweetheart," Lawson crooned before nuzzling his balls, driving Dayne out of his mind. He'd honestly thought he'd never be intimate with anyone again. "You are never boring." Lawson ran his lips up and down Dayne's cock before sucking him into wet heat.

Thinking became a nonissue.

"Lawson…." Dayne quivered and shook as Lawson did things Dayne had only dreamed of. "God… I…."

"Just relax." Lawson smiled and then sucked him again, this time even harder.

Dayne rolled his head back and forth on the pillow, pinching his own nipples for added stimulation. He thrust his hips because he couldn't stop himself, and damned if Lawson didn't meet each thrust, taking all of him. That was hot, and Dayne needed to watch as his cock slipped between Lawson's lips. Even his sometimes-fevered imagination hadn't come up with a sight so unbelievably sexy. He groaned and gave himself over to Lawson, who drove him to the brink and then backed off, only to do it again and again. "Lawson, I…." Dayne swallowed and managed to keep control of himself as Lawson backed away. "That was amazing."

"I think you're the one who's pretty amazing." Lawson crawled up him, brought their lips together as he lay on the bed, then rolled Dayne onto his side and pulled him on top. "This is going to be more comfortable for you."

"Fuck," Dayne groaned as he realized Lawson's entire body was laid out for him. He didn't know where to start first. He explored Lawson's plated chest, teasing his nipples as corded muscle shook under his touch.

"Look what you do to me," Lawson said as he lifted his head, and Dayne followed his gaze to Lawson's leaking cock, lying on his belly. "All I have to do is think about you and that happens. I think of you all the time. At night I've stared up at the ceiling, wondering what it would be like to have you in my bed and my life." Lawson pulled him down into a kiss that curled Dayne's toes.

"But how can you?"

"The heart wants what the heart wants." Lawson cut off further conversation by tugging him down into a kiss as he held Dayne tight. He shifted his hips, and soon their cocks lay side by side, sliding against each other.

Dayne moaned against Lawson's lips and rocked back and forth, loving the whimper Lawson made. To think he was able to make a guy as big and strong as Lawson react that way. It was a keen sense of power. Reactions like that didn't lie—Lawson really was attracted to him. Some of Dayne's doubt slipped away, and he rocked faster, Lawson's cock sliding along Dayne's belly.

"You're a special man, and I hope you give me the chance to keep showing you how special I think you are."

Dayne groaned and arched his back, pressing harder on Lawson's hips as his excitement grew. He was getting close, and judging by his ragged breathing, Lawson was as well. He moved faster, and Lawson moaned and held still. Heat spread between them, slicking the way, and Dayne followed seconds later, crying out as his release barreled into him.

He didn't dare move in case something woke him from this hazy, floaty dream. Dayne was held gently, trying to catch his breath, as the slow realization dawned on him of what they'd done.

"Just lie still." Lawson gently rubbed up and down Dayne's back. For the first time in months, Dayne felt no pain in his legs. It was like everything had been shut off and he was perfect and whole again. He knew that was an illusion, but he'd take it, just like he'd revel in Lawson's bright smile and the warmth of his embrace.

Lawson rolled him on the bed, settling Dayne on his back, and after giving him a soft kiss, he left the bed. He returned with a warm cloth, which he used to clean Dayne's skin, and a soft towel to dry him with. Lawson left and returned again, this time rejoining him in bed.

Dayne rolled onto his side and curled next to Lawson. He wanted to believe things between them were possible, he really did, so he put aside his doubts and worries.

"Sweetheart, I can hear your thoughts churning in your head. Don't worry so much. Sometimes you have to take what happens and enjoy the moment."

"That's hard for me." There had been too many instances for Dayne not to take that idea seriously. "I know it's probably me just being paranoid, but it's happened. And what if something bad happens to you because of me?"

"If something bad does happen, it won't have anything to do with you. Things happen for their own reasons and in their own time. I know it hurts, but your house burning down had nothing to do with you. It was an accident."

"Just like the one that took Jeff and nearly took my legs. Accidents seem to happen to me, and I don't want one of my accidents to hurt you." Dayne rested his head on Lawson's shoulder and closed his eyes. He was not going to let fear run the rest of his life. He told himself that over and over, hoping it would become true.

Chapter 6

LAWSON WAS beyond tired. He stank of sweat, smoke, and charred wood. The weather had been very dry lately, and a family cooking out in their backyard had been careless. They'd actually built a fire in an old wheel, and sparks had gotten in the roof vents and started a fire in the attic. They'd gone to bed not knowing the flames were smoldering.

He pulled up in front of his house after four long shifts and sighed, thankful he had the next three days off. Lawson grabbed his gear and hauled it inside. His stomach growled as soon as he walked in the door and smelled garlic, oregano, and tomato aromas. For the last three nights, Dayne had had something ready for him to eat when he got home.

"You're going to spoil me," Lawson called as he dropped his bag on the rug in the hall. He was too damn tired to carry it any longer.

"I'm still working on the sauce," Dayne said and then swore softly. Lawson had learned that when things didn't go right in the kitchen, Dayne could swear fast enough and loud enough to make a sailor blush down to his toes. "I'll have things ready for you in fifteen minutes."

Lawson went into the kitchen, which looked like a spaghetti sauce bomb had gone off in it, and saw Dayne frantically cleaning up the spatter. He chuckled and kissed Dayne, his nervous flutters settling. "You're too good to me." He left the room and carried his gear downstairs. Then he started the washing machine and stripped out of his clothes, threw everything he could in to be cleaned, and padded up the stairs in his boxers.

Dayne wolf-whistled as Lawson passed the kitchen door. "Hot stuff."

It was so good to see Dayne laugh and joke. That part of his personality had started coming out just a few days ago, and it was awesome. Lawson hurried on up the stairs and into the bathroom to wash the stink off him. He shucked his boxers and started the water. After a day like today, his muscles hurt. It had been one call after another, and his arms and shoulders ached.

The hot water was amazing, and Lawson stood under the spray, just letting it run over him. The tension he'd been carrying sluiced down the drain along with the water, and once he could move again, Lawson started soaping himself up. He closed his eyes and imagined Dayne in here with him. They hadn't showered together yet, and it was an experience Lawson was looking forward to. Wet Dayne had to be something spectacular, and shower sex was awesome. Though Lawson would need to be careful with Dayne's legs, he knew it would be hot.

"Lawson." Dayne tapped on the door. "Dinner is nearly ready."

Lawson was already gripping his cock and stopped his hand midstroke. This wasn't a good idea. Not when he had the real object of his desire right outside the door. "I'll be done in a few minutes." He rinsed, turned off the water, got out, dried himself, and hurried to his room in only a towel.

Dressed in an old concert T-shirt and a pair of light sweatpants, he met Dayne in the kitchen, where a sumptuous feast was waiting for him. The room smelled amazing, and Dayne was already making up his plate. "I have bread too." He hurried to the oven, and the scent of garlicky butteriness filled the room.

"You rock." Lawson took a piece of bread when Dayne brought it over, and bit into the hot, warm goodness. "How did you know I loved this?"

"Just lucky." Dayne sat and made up his own—considerably less full—plate. "My mom used to make great spaghetti sauce. She got the recipe from a church cookbook that she found at a rummage sale, and she taught me how to do it." Dayne grew quiet and set down his fork. He turned away. Lawson wondered what was wrong until he replayed what Dayne had said. That church cookbook, the one that had provided the end result of this meal, had been lost in the fire at Dayne's. "I'm sorry for being such a baby."

"You know it's okay." It was on the tip of his tongue to say something to try to make Dayne feel better, but he had nothing but platitudes, which weren't going to help. Lawson patted Dayne's hand to let him know he understood and then gave him a few minutes to get himself together. "How was class today?"

"Good. I turned in my paper in my American studies class on reading the romance, and the instructor had a friend come in who writes romances. We had a really lively discussion. It was pretty awesome. She was a grandmother of three and incredibly knowledgeable about the business."

"Have you had time to get back to your research on the school?" Lawson rolled spaghetti around his fork and took a bite, then hummed his approval.

"Not much. I've been busy with other things, but I was going to go through that diary some more. Did I tell you they had their first kiss? I read that a few days ago. It's a real-life love story, and I've been anxious to know what happens next."

"Then why haven't you read more?"

Dayne took a bite of garlic bread. "I think I wanted to share it with you."

Lawson continued eating and smiled. "Okay. Let me finish eating, and then we can look over the diary together." He wasn't sure how much longer he was going to be able to stay awake, but he wanted to make Dayne happy.

"I have strawberry shortcake for dessert."

"Man." Lawson was getting majorly spoiled. He ate everything Dayne had put on his plate and brought it to the sink. He loaded the dishwasher and helped Dayne clean up. Then they went into the living room and sat on the couch, with Tati settling on his lap for a change.

Lawson leaned back, and Dayne opened the diary.

"February 14, 1909

"Today is Valentine's Day, and even though it's a White man's holiday, the girls and even some of the boys have made hearts for the ones they're sweet on. That's how they put it. I made a heart out of red paper, but I left it blank and put it in one of Matthew's books. I didn't sign it, and I hoped he would know it's from me and that no one else will notice. They didn't seem to, and I saw Matthew find it and look it over. Then he smiled. Matthew looked at me slyly and then put the heart back in his book.

"Matthew saw me after classes and before supper, and he thanked me for the Valentine. He doesn't understand the holiday any more than I do, but he smiled at me and we went for a walk in the woods behind the school. There was no one around, and Matthew kissed me again, this time with more passion, and I held him close. It was exciting. We heard someone else near us and pulled away. Matthew hurried deeper into the forest, and I walked back toward the school, passing Johnny Longbow on the way. He smiled and winked at me.

"I don't know if Johnny knows or suspects that Matthew and I were together. He hasn't said anything, and Matthew came back on his own fifteen minutes later and was almost late for dinner. I watched Matthew during prayers, and then we had free time. Matthew sat next to me, and we talked about school and our assignments. Neither of us mentioned anything about what happened in the woods, and I don't know if Matthew is trying to pretend it never happened. I'm scared to ask him about it.

"I found a red heart, like the one I had made Matthew, under the cover of my math book. Like mine, it wasn't signed, but I know it was from Matthew. After study time, we went to bed, and I'm writing this late at night because it's the only time I get when there isn't someone looking over my shoulder.

"Someone's coming and I have to hide the book."

Dayne closed the book. "The entry ends there. I read that he found a secure place, but I don't know where it is." He shifted on the sofa, bumping Lawson's shoulder. "Are you asleep?"

"No." Lawson didn't open his eyes. "I was listening. I love the way you read. It's so expressive and gentle."

Dayne stood. "Come on. You need to go to bed and get some rest. We can read some more in the morning. You're barely staying awake, and tomorrow you can sleep in and do what you do on your day off."

Lawson yawned. "I thought I'd take you over to your classes. Maybe we could have lunch, and I'll walk around town while you're busy."

"You don't have to."

Lawson sat up and tugged Dayne down into his arms. "Maybe I want to spend a little time with you." He lay back down with Dayne on top of him. "I could hold you like this forever." He closed his eyes once again, the fresh scent of Dayne's hair in his nose, and he was happy. This was what life should be. He jumped out of airplanes and ran into burning buildings, but maybe he'd been searching for this, something simple and special, and looking in the wrong places.

"Then let's go upstairs. You're comfortable enough, but your back is going to be killing you in the morning if you stay like this for very long."

"I don't want to move." He was surprisingly comfortable and closed his eyes once again. He knew he had to shift, and groaned when Dayne got up. He noticed Dayne was walking stiffly, so once he stood, Lawson took Dayne's hand and climbed the stairs with him, turning out the lights as they went. Lawson didn't want to make a big deal of it, but this was his way of helping Dayne up the stairs without Dayne knowing.

They took turns in the bathroom, and Lawson practically fell into bed. He had intended to make love to Dayne, but he was too worn out, and after kissing Dayne good night and settling his head on the pillow, he was out for the count.

IN THE morning, Lawson felt Dayne getting out of the bed and kept his eyes closed when Dayne groaned softly and headed for the bathroom. Lawson stayed in bed until Dayne returned, and then he took his turn while Dayne dressed.

"Do you want some breakfast?"

Lawson checked his watch. "There's a great little coffee shop near the campus, if I remember correctly. What time is your first class?"

"Eleven."

"Then let's go, and I'll buy you breakfast." Lawson waited as Dayne grabbed his things.

"You know, I'm capable of taking care of myself." Dayne finished getting his backpack ready and walked slowly toward the front door.

Lawson opened the coat closet and handed Dayne his cane. Dayne looked about ready to murder him right there on the spot. "There's no shame in needing some help." He leaned closer. "Besides, I don't want you so worn out that once you're done with class, you and I can't have some fun of our own."

"So this is all about you?" Dayne grinned but didn't hand the cane back.

"You're hurting. I can see it, and I know you're feeling it." Lawson wondered when the last time Dayne had been to see a doctor was. This amount of chronic pain couldn't be right. There had to be something they could do for him.

"I... I...." Dayne stopped what he was going to say.

"I only want you to feel better. That's all." This was an ego thing for Dayne, but if it meant getting around easier and with less pain, Lawson was all for it.

"You really want to be seen with an old man?"

Lawson honestly had never thought of it that way. "I want to be seen with you in any form. Cane or not, limp or not. It doesn't matter to me other than when you're moving extra stiffly, so I know you're in pain, and that bothers me. Cane good, pain bad." As far as he was concerned, that was all there was to it. "I was on crutches until the gash in my side healed, because they needed to keep my leg stable. I know what it feels like to need help."

"You don't know what it looks like to walk into college classes using a cane."

"So you're saying that the people in wheelchairs have something to be ashamed of?" Lawson put his hands on his hips. He knew he was pushing the issue, but he wanted to make his point.

"Of course not. But…."

"I know. They don't to you. You don't see anything wrong with anyone else doing what they have to. It's that you want to be as normal as possible. Well, build a bridge, get over it, and do what will give your legs a rest."

"Piss off." Dayne sounded really testy.

"No. If I didn't give a shit, I wouldn't say anything." He opened the front door, and Dayne used his cane to go out to the car. Lawson locked the door behind them, unlocked the car, opened the door for Dayne, and then went around to get in the car.

"I know you're trying to help me," Dayne said after Lawson turned onto the street. "It's hard. I like to think of myself as whole and…."

"You are whole." Lawson pulled to a stop at the stop sign. Dayne didn't argue with him, which worried Lawson a little. He'd feel better if Dayne would fight with him and explain what he was thinking. "You're an impressive man, and that's all there is to it."

"Yeah. I can't even run."

"So what? I can run damn well, but I can't do the things you're doing. I'm not a college man. I'm a firefighter, period. That's all I know and all I'm good at. You can do damn near anything you want. So who cares if you have trouble getting around sometimes." Lawson made the turn and started out of town, heading west.

"But you're not the one who has trouble walking."

"No. But as a kid, I was the one who couldn't sit still in class and was on medication that the kids found out about and picked on me for. I had a lot of trouble learning to read, and the solution was for me to get glasses. Ugly, awful glasses that I got picked on for too. So if we had to trade places, I think I'd choose what you have. I'd like to be smart enough to be able to go to college like you."

"But...."

Lawson gently placed his hand on Dayne's leg. "I just want you to know that I think you're pretty amazing, cane or not."

"You really feel that way?" Dayne asked after a few seconds.

"Of course I do. I'm not shallow." Lawson tried not to sound offended. Guys often looked at him and thought he had the depth of an overturned saucer, and that bothered him. When he saw people, he was willing to look beyond the outer appearance.

"I know you aren't. But it's hard to believe the good things right now." Dayne turned to look out the passenger window, and Lawson let him take the time he needed.

Lawson entered the freeway and picked up speed, joining the traffic on 81 going west. He got off at High Street in Carlisle, went through town, and parked in front of the coffee shop. They went inside, with Dayne using his cane, and no one paid any attention to him other than the girl who took his order, because she nearly tripped over the cane. She repositioned it for Dayne and moved on. It was one of those "I told you so" moments. Lawson remained quiet, and they ate a nice breakfast.

One of the things he liked about being with Dayne was that neither of them seemed to feel it necessary to fill every second with talking. They could sit at breakfast, be together, and not talk. Lawson was still going through the wake-up process, and the first cup of coffee the server brought him disappeared pretty quickly, and he ordered another, feeling much more awake and alert. "We have a little while before your class."

"I usually go to the library to work." Dayne pulled out one of his books. "Is it okay if I review things before the class?"

"You do whatever you need to." Lawson sat back, watching Dayne and drinking his coffee. He had always been an on-the-go kind of guy. On vacation he loved activities and packed in as much to see as possible. But with Dayne he was discovering the pleasure in quiet time with someone else. He was relaxing. His life was filled with pressures, and he'd always handled it by trying to escape from them by adding even more excitement. Sure, he still wanted action and adventure, but having some downtime was also showing its benefit. "I saw a candy store a little ways back. I'm going to walk down there and see if they have anything interesting. I won't be long." He finished his coffee and lightly touched Dayne's shoulder before leaving the shop.

He passed a group of guys talking animatedly to each other, and they stopped as he went by. Lawson smiled as he imagined them turning to look at him as he went. He'd seen those looks before and knew exactly what they meant.

In the candy store, he was a little overwhelmed. They had all the candy he remembered as a kid. Not that he was particularly hungry for anything. He ended up with a pack of sour gummy bears because sweet and sour together were awesome.

"Hi," said one of the guys he'd passed earlier when Lawson grabbed a second bag of candy and was about to go to the register. "You're something else." He was a small blond with guyliner and full lips who obviously knew how he looked and what he could get away with. "I saw you watching and was wondering if you like to do more than look."

"Excuse me?" Guys usually weren't this forward outside of a club. Lawson smiled, but tried not to show any outright encouragement.

"You're superhot, and I told my friends I was going to come over and talk to you. They said I didn't have the balls."

"So you talking to me was a bet?"

"No." He flashed a million-watt megasmile. "I would have come to talk to you if they hadn't said anything. I'm not one of those quiet queens who sits back and prays to be seen. I get out and go for it." He snapped his fingers once and struck a pose, just for a second, but enough to be eye-catching.

"Well, thank you. But I have someone I'm with back at the coffee shop." Lawson paid for his purchase and left the store. It wasn't long before he heard the small gaggle of guys following him.

"I bet his boyfriend is super-cute-hot," one of the guys said. Lawson figured he wasn't supposed to hear that and smiled to himself.

At the coffee shop, he went inside, where Dayne was nose-deep in his book. "It's quarter to eleven." He sat next to Dayne and handed him one of the packages of candy.

"What's this?"

"A snack for you if you need it." Lawson tucked the package into Dayne's bag and saw the four guys outside, talking to each other and nodding. They must have thought Dayne was cute-hot too. Lawson ignored them and took Dayne's pack while he got up, leaning on his cane. Lawson held the door, and they walked past the small group to the car.

"Why are they staring at me?" Dayne asked as he got in the car.

"One of them talked to me at the store," Lawson said after he got in. "I think he was curious if I was into guyliner. For the record, it's okay, but not necessary and way too much effort." Lawson pulled out and drove to the building where Dayne said he had class.

"They were cute," Dayne said. "I see them around campus. They're part of the 'out in your face' crowd. The unapologetically gay crowd. They call other guys *darling*...." The growl in his voice told Lawson something. He suspected Dayne desperately wanted to have that kind of confidence and instead was intimidated by them.

"They have nothing on you." Lawson parked and waited for Dayne to get his things. "I'll see you in a little over an hour, and we can have lunch or something."

"You don't have to wait for me. I have this class, and then my next one today is at two. You don't have to waste your entire day sitting around here waiting for me."

"I won't. I'm going to the library in town for a while. Just have a good class and don't worry about me. I'll be fine." Lawson smiled and watched as Dayne went inside. Then he pulled away and drove around the block to the library. He parked again and went inside.

He went to the card catalog and asked one of the librarians for help in finding books about the Carlisle Indian Industrial School. They had a few, and he spent some time looking through them for any reference to his great-great-uncle. There were none, but he had to try. A few of the books contained lists of students by class, but they were all English names and Lawson only knew the name the tribe used. He kept hoping someone kept records of the various names and a cross-reference, but he wasn't finding it.

"Thank you for your help."

"Did you find what you were looking for?" the dark-haired librarian asked in her calm voice.

"No."

"Try at Dickinson. They have a lot of the records there, as well as at the historical society. My guess is that if what you're looking for exists, those are your best chances to find it."

"Thank you." He gave her a smile and left. He'd already checked both places and come up with nothing. Lawson was quickly realizing the information he sought probably didn't exist any longer. If it ever had in the first place.

Lawson walked the half block to where Dayne's class was and met him as he came out of the building, scowling under a head of steam. "What's going on?"

"Some girl asked me if I was using my cane to get attention or something," Dayne said. "I wanted to punch her."

"I'm surprised the college tolerates behavior like that."

"They aren't supposed to, but the professor was right there and didn't do anything." Dayne leaned on his cane, lines etched around his mouth. "I'm not sure what to do. It was one stupid comment from one airhead, but...."

Lawson understood. It was like pressing one of Dayne's buttons, especially when he'd been feeling insecure already. Lawson wanted to go inside, find the professor, and give him a piece of his mind. But Dayne was perfectly able to stand up for himself and didn't need Lawson to fight his battles. "Go on inside and take care of it. I'll wait for you if you like."

"But you've already been waiting for me, and...." Dayne bit his lower lip.

"And we have two hours for lunch. Take care of what you need to." Lawson walked up the steps and opened the front door. Dayne went inside, and Lawson followed and took a seat on one of the chairs in the entry hall.

The building was over a hundred years old, with wooden staircases and banisters that had been polished by thousands of hands. The scuffed paneled walls had seen decades of students and gave the entire area a warm, settled tone.

"Dayne," a man called as he raced down the stairs to meet him. "I was told what someone said to you." The young, balding man turned to Lawson, who got up and walked to where Dayne stood on the stairs.

"Yes. Sheila wasn't particularly flattering."

"The college doesn't tolerate that kind of talk. We classify it as hate speech, and she will be spoken to. But I was concerned about you. This is the first time you've used the cane. Are you all right?"

"Yes. My legs sometimes hurt, and.... Professor Mather, this is my friend Lawson.... He suggested I use the cane to give them a rest. I don't like to use it...."

"You should feel free to use whatever you need to. There is an elevator in the back of the building. If that makes things easier, then please use it, and if you need any assistance, let any of the faculty know. We'll all be here to help."

"I just don't want to feel self-conscious."

"And there's no reason you should. We have students with artificial limbs, in wheelchairs, and those who need daily assistance.

This institution is dedicated to improving the mind as well as the spirits and horizons of our students—all our students."

"Thank you." Dayne slowly made his way back down the stairs. "I didn't want to make waves. I'm only here for the semester and don't want to cause anyone trouble."

Professor Mather's expression grew more serious. "I want you to come talk to me about that. I think that you would make a real asset to the Dickinson student community. Please come see me when you can so we can talk further. Good to meet you, Lawson." He turned and went up the stairs.

Dayne leaned into Lawson's arms as he reached the bottom of the stairs. "The Hub is just down there. It's a sandwich shop."

"Can you walk that far?"

"I'm not an invalid, and my legs are loosening up now."

Lawson wasn't sure if Dayne was making light of things or not, but they walked to the shop and climbed the stairs. The Hub was located in what had once been a large home, and they had seating on the wraparound porch, as well as inside. Dayne got porch seats for them, and after finding out what Dayne wanted, Lawson went inside to order.

"Well, if it isn't my lucky day." It was the kid from the candy store, minus his friends. "Is that your boyfriend? Is he a student here?"

"We're working on it." Lawson turned to where he could see the top of Dayne's head through the window.

"Damn…," the kid said as Lawson turned back to him. "I'd give just about anything to have someone smile at me like that."

Lawson got in line and placed their orders, then stepped aside to wait. When the food was ready, he grabbed the tray and carried it out to where Dayne waited.

It was a glorious fall day, with a slight nip in the air, but it was clear and smelled clean and fresh, with the heavy humidity of summer becoming a thing of the past. Everyone seemed to have had the same idea, because the porch was packed, with the only open chairs at their table.

The kid who'd been waiting behind him came out, looking around. Lawson felt a little sorry for him and waved. He smiled and hurried over. "Thanks. I'm Bobby."

"Lawson, and this is Dayne." They shook hands, and Bobby sat.

"I haven't seen you around before. You look a little old to be a freshman, so did you transfer in or start late?"

"I'm a junior, and I'm here for the semester on a special program studying education. What about you?" Dayne glanced questioningly at Lawson, and he gave Dayne a smile and a gentle pat on the leg. He was only being nice.

"Liberal arts. This is my sophomore year, and I still don't know what I want to do. So many of my classes are the general ed type anyway, but I need to get my tush in gear and figure it out before my dad blows a circuit and decides he doesn't want to pay for tuition any longer. Not that Mom is really going to let him do that, but he wants me to make a decision and stick with it." Bobby finally took a bite and quieted while he chewed. As soon as he swallowed, he was off to the races again. "Did you hurt your leg? I saw you using a cane. I hope everything is okay."

It was like having lunch with the Energizer Bunny. "I was in an accident a few years ago that left my legs messed up. Some days I'm fine, while others I need a little help. But it's good."

"That's so awesome. The soldiering on, I mean. I never let anything get me down. Not when I decided to go here instead of UVA like Dad did, or when I told Mom and Dad I was gay and they wondered if they could have me fixed. That's how Dad put it—the same word he used with the dog."

Lawson chuckled. "What did you say?" As if he couldn't imagine.

"I told them that I was perfectly fine as I was and that all this fabulousness didn't need to be fixed, thank you very much, and then I called Gramps, and he explained things to them, and everything was okay after that. No one argues with him, ever. They still don't understand me, but that's okay. I can live with that." He took another bite and lowered his gaze. "Sorry. I always talk way too much." He turned his gaze to Lawson. "What do you do?"

"I'm a fireman."

Bobby's mouth fell open. "No way. That's awesome, and you sure look like one of those fantasy firemen on the calendars you see in the stores."

"He was in one of those," Dayne said. "I've been trying to find a copy and can't. It was a few years ago. Apparently he was Mr. July." He smiled, eyes flashing.

"Oh my gawd! A calendar guy." Bobby looked like he'd won the lottery. "How did you meet?"

"I saw him first at the historical society, and then he was there when my house burned down and helped me." Dayne leaned against his arm.

"No way! Really?" The way he said it made Lawson wonder if Bobby was contemplating setting a fire just so he could see how many hunky firemen showed up.

"Yeah. Lawson's been amazing." Dayne returned to his sandwich.

Lawson ate as well, while Bobby chattered on about everything that caught his eye. Lawson half expected him to wax poetic about the leaves as they fell from the trees.

"I'm going to prepare for my next class if that's okay," Dayne said as he finished eating and pulled out a book.

"Of course it is." Lawson got another drink and sat quietly while Dayne worked. Bobby had to rush off to his next class, and Lawson just relaxed for a few minutes. He needed something to do, so he got out his phone, pulled up a mindless game, and crushed some candy. Once Dayne was ready, he walked him back to class. "I'll be here when you're ready to go."

"Lawson, it's nice that you came with me, but you don't have to waste your time like this."

"This isn't a waste of time, and tomorrow I have a full day with appointments, and in the afternoon, I'm joining a jump class, so I wanted to spend time with you today."

"Oh."

"Don't worry. I shouldn't be too late." He knew Dayne was nervous about the skydiving. "You worry so much. I've been diving for years now. I like it, and I'm helping other people have fun. Last time I helped a seventy-five-year-old man take his first jump. It was amazing."

"If you say so." Dayne walked up to the door of the building, and Lawson pulled it open for him. "It's just that I'll never be able to do that."

"So?"

"How will I keep you interested?"

They were back to that. Lawson stopped. "Let's say that we're together for thirty years. Do you think we'll do everything together? There will be things you like and things I like, as well as things we'll do as a couple. It's okay to have separate interests." He wasn't sure if Dayne understood what he was trying to say or not. He hoped so.

They said good-bye, and Lawson spent the next hour wandering around the area. Then he met Dayne as he came out of the building.

"Let me go get the car and I'll be right back." He hurried away toward where he'd parked, then pulled up to where Dayne was waiting.

Dayne was on the phone but held open the door and got inside, then sighed when he was able to sit down. "Thank you. So I don't need to try to make a list of everything? ... I see. ... All right, then. Yes...." Dayne shut the door and placed his cane in the backseat. "So that's the end of it?" A tear ran down Dayne's cheek, and he swiped it away. "Then I'll look for the check." Lawson shifted to pull out his wallet and handed Dayne one of his personal cards. Dayne read the address off, then listened for a few minutes more. "I don't need to sign anything over to you? ... Okay, I see. ... Okay. I can meet them there when you schedule it." Dayne listened some more and then hung up, slumping in the seat like a rag doll.

"What is it?" Lawson didn't try to piece together the parts of the conversation. He put the car in gear and started for home.

"They've declared the house a total loss and are going to pay me the full amounts on the policy for both the house and the contents. They also said they would have people out to demolish the rest of the house. Apparently the borough has rules about things like that. I still own the property, and they aren't doing anything with the garage. So pretty soon I'll own a small piece of land with a garage on it and a filled-in hole. Everything I owned is now a garage and an otherwise empty lot." Dayne put his hands over his face.

"You could rebuild."

"Nope. He said the house doesn't meet current setbacks or some such crap. That's why they're going to fill it in. So I'd have to build a different house, and who knows what that's going to cost." Dayne sighed. "I don't know what I'm going to do."

"How about make decisions when you're feeling better? They're sending you a check, so put it in the bank and think about what you want to do."

"I can't just stay with you forever."

"You can do whatever you need to. All I'm saying is, give yourself a chance to breathe and make the decisions you need to when you aren't feeling quite so vulnerable." Lawson turned onto the freeway, heading toward home.

Dayne didn't talk much, spending his time looking out the window. Lawson turned on the radio to listen to music as he drove, letting Dayne think. This whole situation made Lawson angry, but he had to remember it was the fact that Dayne's house burned down that allowed them to really meet. So while he didn't want Dayne hurting, the incident causing the pain was ultimately bringing Lawson some happiness. Sometimes life wasn't fair.

"Can we go by my house… or what's left of it?" Dayne asked as they got off the freeway, and Lawson drove them over.

There wasn't much left at all, and a recent rain had turned the area around the house into a dried-up soup of ash and bits of charred wood. They got out and walked around what little remained of the structure, which still smelled burned. Dayne slowly descended the first stairs to the basement.

"Do you think that's a good idea?" Lawson worried that with Dayne's legs hurting, more stairs were going to make things worse.

Dayne ignored him and continued the rest of the way down, and Lawson followed him. Peeks of evening sun shone through the gaps in the floor above. Streaks of light in an otherwise dank place.

"There's nothing left down here." Dayne stood in front of the melted shelves. "I was hoping something might have been usable. But I should have known." He turned back toward the stairs. "I keep hoping to find some stash, something the flames missed, but except for the dressers, they were very efficient."

Dayne started climbing the stairs and faltered, knees buckling like he was going to fall.

Lawson raced over, caught him, and carried him out into the sunlight, his cane tumbling back down the stairs. Lawson placed Dayne on the grass and returned for his cane, then handed it to him and helped him up. "Let's go home."

"I want to check the garage."

"I'll do that for you. Is there anything out of it that you want?"

"Not really. We didn't keep a bunch of things out there. It was mostly where I parked my car. I just wanted to make sure it was still secure and someone hadn't broken in or anything."

Lawson hurried out and checked the doors, making sure everything looked all right. Then he returned to Dayne, helped him to the car, and drove to his place. "Does this kind of thing happen very often?"

"No."

"Then please call your doctor." He placed his hand on Dayne's leg, the muscles spasming under his hand. "Just to have him check things over."

"I have bad days every now and then." Dayne got out of the car and stood as tall as he could as he walked to the house. "I'm not an invalid or something."

Lawson wanted to swear, but he kept his temper. He could see the pain Dayne was experiencing in each step he took. "I didn't say you were, but you're hurting." God, that was so hard to witness. Not to mention the fact that Lawson had stopped him from falling back down the stairs.

"I'm fine."

"What you are is a stubborn ass," Lawson countered.

"And you're a jerk who thinks he knows what's best for everyone else," Dayne challenged, his jaw set and eyes hard as granite.

"That's probably true, but only because I'm usually right." He tilted his eyebrows, and Dayne groaned. "See."

"Fine. I'll call the doctor and have him look me over. But if he wants to poke at shit, I'm going to make you pay." Dayne glared and then turned away. "I've had enough of doctors to last me the rest of my life."

Dayne followed him inside, and Lawson waited while Dayne made an appointment.

"Was that so hard?"

"Bastard!" Dayne shuffled into the living room and collapsed onto the sofa.

"You can call me whatever you want as long as you find out what's going on." Lawson sat in the chair while Dayne looked at anything in the room but him. "You already know."

"Yeah. And I know they're going to want to do more surgery, and I've been through so much already. I don't think I can do more cutting and then the weeks in a chair and months more rehab and therapy. I've been through that routine more times than I can count. I don't want to do it all again." Dayne looked tired and his eyes drooped.

"Can I get you something?"

Dayne shook his head. "I have pain pills, but they knock me out, so I'll take one before I go to bed so I can sleep. I've done that before, and I'm sure it won't be the last time." He stood, using his cane, and slowly left the room. "I got some steaks on sale at the store yesterday on my way home, so I thought we could have those."

Lawson jumped up. "I can make dinner."

Dayne shook his head. "Look, you let me stay with you, so the least I can do is make you dinner. I'm not helpless."

Lawson gave in and went back into the living room. He need to let Dayne do things for himself no matter how much he wanted to step in. He knew from his training that sometimes people resisted help when they might need it the most, and all he could do was let Dayne be Dayne. Instead, he went down to the basement to put in another load of laundry. It was funny, but it seemed that two people in the house made three times as much dirty clothes.

Tati wound her way around his legs, then sat down, blinking at him. "I know. He's having a hard time right now. It probably won't last too long." He finished and went back upstairs.

The kitchen was surprisingly quiet, and when he peeked inside, Dayne was sitting at the table, making salad. Seasoned steaks rested on a plate on the counter. "Do you have a grill?"

"Of course. Do you want me to take care of those?"

"Would you?" Dayne sounded so small. "I'm sorry for being a problem. I just can't go through what they're going to tell me needs to be done."

"You won't know until you go to the doctor."

"Yes, I do. They already told me the last time I saw them. They said that they needed to correct the ligaments in my knee or the pain was going to get worse, though for a while it didn't. I actually thought they were wrong. My knees stopped hurting, and I didn't need the cane."

"Just see what they have to say. Today could have been a bad day and things are improving." Lawson wanted everything to be all right.

"I hope so, but I'm scared." Dayne turned away and went back to what he was doing.

111

Lawson went outside, lit the grill, and used the brush to clean the grates. He knew fear when he saw it, and Dayne was terrified. He closed the lid on the grill and went back inside.

Dayne sat at the table, knife still, halfway through the tomato he'd been cutting for dinner. "I'm such a loser. I should be able to face this. I've been through worse."

"Dayne…." Lawson placed his hands on Dayne's shoulders.

"What if they want to take my legs?" Dayne choked out. "What if they can't do anything for me and it's too late? They always told me that was a possibility and that I beat the odds before. With my luck, it's caught up to me." Dayne put his hand over Lawson's and squeezed tightly. "I don't know what I'll do if that happens."

"You'll do what you've always done—move forward." Lawson leaned down and held him. "Maybe you're letting yourself get too far ahead. Just try to relax and not worry about it too much. I mean, isn't it better to know than to worry about what it could be?"

"Yeah." Dayne leaned against his hand and then let go and finished cutting the tomato. "I'll be fine. I need to calm down and stop worrying."

"You sure?"

Dayne nodded, and Lawson grabbed the plate of steaks and went back to the grill. Dayne had been through a lot, and maybe he had a reason to worry. But Lawson thought maybe he was blowing things out of proportion and he might need to rest his legs for a while. Hopefully the doctor would have some answers for him that would put Dayne's mind to rest. God, Lawson certainly hoped so. If anyone deserved a break, it was Dayne.

He grilled the steaks and brought them in when they were wonderfully medium. Dayne had put out plates, and Lawson placed a steak on each one, then carried them into the living room, intending to watch television.

"I read something today that I want to share with you after dinner," Dayne said.

"Okay." Lawson turned on *The Big Bang Theory*, and they ate while laughing at Sheldon's antics. "I think I'd smack him at least once an hour."

"Yeah. But he does it to himself. That's what's so funny." It was nice to see Dayne relax and laugh for a while, but the worry was still there under the surface.

"It is, and he usually gets it in the end." Lawson smiled and sat back as the episode ended. He'd finished his dinner, so he took the dishes to the kitchen, knowing if he didn't, Dayne would. When he returned, he took care of Dayne's as well, loaded the dishwasher, and brought two Sam Adams back with him.

"Thanks." Dayne took the bottle and set it aside.

Chapter 7

"*MARCH 21, 1909*

"*Spring is finally arriving and I am no longer cold all the time. The White man clothes for winter don't keep out the chill, and the dormitories are drafty and cold. For months the wind has blown through, rattling windows, and I kept wondering why the White men were not smart enough to put skins over them. And they think we don't know anything.*"

Dayne paused. He could see Ted rolling his eyes as he wrote the entry.

"*The sun is warming. The snow, which was heavy, has melted away, and everything outside is caked with mud. It was all I could do not to rush outside first thing in the morning, but getting muddy and tracking dirt inside is cause for punishment. Like anyone can stop the earth from getting anywhere.*

"*After classes and before dinner, Matthew and I went into the bare woods. The trees towered overhead, the ground drying, and we walked farther away from the school. I asked Matthew if he ever thought of running away from here. He said he thinks about it all the time. Matthew hates school. He has a hard time learning English, and the teachers are not helping. So as much as we can, he and I spend time together so he can try to learn. The White man's language is hard. Sometimes it's like they talk in code and Matthew doesn't have the key. Today we spoke in our tongue.*

"*Matthew told me how much he's appreciated what I've done for him, and then he kissed me like he has before. It was so gentle and caring. The thrill of touching him was almost too much. Matthew is my best friend, and I know I am growing to love him the way most men love women. What's between Matthew and me is too great and wonderful to keep to myself, so I found a better hiding place for my thoughts. There's a vent in the wall behind my bed, and I keep this there, locked away where no one else can find it. I can't write as much as I like, because I don't want anyone to hear me hiding my book, but I had to write today because things were too exciting for me not to tell.*

"I am scared what will happen if anyone finds out about us, and I am prepared to run away home rather than stay and face what the White man calls justice. They don't know what the word means, even though it is their own. But I cannot run as long as Matthew is here. So I stay to be with him.

"Maybe he and I can run away together when the time comes. But right now we have no food or supplies, and the weather is still too cold to go with only White man clothes, so we will stay here until the time is right, and then I hope he and I will go together."

Dayne closed his eyes briefly. "They're like two wild beings caught in a cage when they should be free. I liked school when I was growing up, but I knew a kid like Ted. He was the first one to run out at the end of school, and he stayed away from the others, walking near the trees. We thought him strange, but I think he needed to be free." Dayne couldn't help feeling for Ted, and he'd hoped that by now Ted might have settled into the school. Maybe the kids never did and that was the problem. The school had taken too much away from them.

"It sounds awful. I hope my great-great-uncle got away."

"What do you know about him?"

"His real name was Soaring Eagle, and according to family stories, he went to the school. But there are no records of that name, and I'm sure he was given an English name, but I don't know what it was. Apparently, when he returned from the school, he was unhappy and broken. My grandmother told us about how, when he was older, he spent months in the woods and stayed away from people for a long time. When he did rejoin the family, he stayed for a few months and then left again."

"Do you think he returned to the school? We might see if there are students who left and returned about that time, if you know what years it was."

"My grandmother said it was between 1908 and 1910. She couldn't remember exactly and said she could be off as well. That's what makes the diary so fascinating. It's possible that Ted and Matthew might have known my great-great-uncle. I don't know. I always got the impression that he didn't return to the school because he hated it so much."

"I'm sorry. I wish I could help you. I will keep an eye out for any reference to the name and see if I come up with anything. Sometimes when you review original documents like this, surprises happen. Tomorrow between classes I'm going to review what Dickinson has, and I may find something for you." Lawson nodded, and Dayne set the diary aside and wound his arms around Lawson's neck. "I think we're both about ready for bed." Dayne pulled him closer.

"Aren't you too tired?"

"Not for this." Dayne took Lawson's lips, kissing hard, letting the pleasure between them blot away the pain in his legs and everything else. "Make me forget."

"As long as you remember me." Lawson stood, taking Dayne with him. He carried Dayne up to the bedroom. Dayne was a little excited, and so were other things, especially with Lawson kissing him as they went.

God, the sensation was heady, and Lawson made it to the bedroom and got Dayne down on the mattress without breaking the hold between them. "Damn, I love the way you feel." Dayne wriggled against him, and Lawson pulled off his shirt before working on Dayne's. But Lawson got sidetracked and sucked at one of Dayne's nipples, sending his head spinning. Lawson was like an octopus, all hands everywhere. Dayne wasn't sure where to concentrate. Somehow

Lawson stopped long enough to get Dayne's shirt off, and then they were chest to chest, skin to skin. Dayne vibrated against him. It was exhilarating beyond belief.

Sex was something Dayne enjoyed, both fun and exciting, but being with Lawson was different. It always seemed as though Dayne was the center of the world and Lawson couldn't get enough of him. To be wanted that much was as head-spinning and flattering as anything Dayne could think of. It only inflamed him, and he needed more.

"God. You need to give me a minute to catch my breath."

Lawson backed away, carefully tugging off Dayne's shoes. He was so caring and gentle, getting the rest of Dayne's clothes off.

Dayne scooted up on the bed so he was more comfortable, watching as Lawson slipped off his jeans and then his underwear, standing in front of him, Lawson junior pointing the way. Only Lawson junior wasn't so little, and as he climbed on the bed, Dayne's throat went dry.

Each movement was feral, like Dayne was being stalked, the heat in Lawson's eyes unmistakable, pupils dilated and huge. Dayne shivered at being the object of Lawson's intense desire. There had to be a mistake, or he had to be dreaming. That was it. This was a dream, and he was going to wake any moment. Lawson wanting him this intensely was too much to hope for.

"You're thinking too much. I can see it in your eyes." Lawson tilted his head, bringing their lips together, and the thinking portion of Dayne's mind flicked off, leaving only what he felt and the heady sensation of clouds and light. That's what Lawson was, sun and light to Dayne's usual dark and night, which was exactly what he needed. With Lawson, everything was just as it should be, and that's what scared him most of the time. But at this moment, all that mattered was Lawson's lips on his belly, licking and sucking, down, down, until his eyes crossed on their own.

Lawson teased him to the point that Dayne humped the air to get a little more sensation. Need replaced everything else as Dayne clung to Lawson, holding him around the neck, the world narrowing to just the two of them. Then Lawson stopped. "What do you want, sweetheart?"

Dayne closed his eyes, breathing through his mouth as he let the cloud dissipate from his mind. "No one since the accident has...." God, he felt like such an ugly duckling.

Lawson stilled. "I don't want to hurt you." The fear in his eyes was exactly what Dayne had been expecting. Everyone saw him as fragile, and in a man, that wasn't attractive. They saw him as needing help and unable to do things for himself, especially with the damn cane, and now Lawson had seen him using the thing and thought the same way.

"I'm not glass, you know. I'm a man just like you." Damn it, this was so hard. He was not going to beg Lawson to be with him that way. If he didn't want that, then Dayne sure as hell wasn't going to insist he join with him. He turned away, ready to give up and let the whole thing go.

"I never thought anything different." Lawson lay next to him, drawing him closer, pressing against his back. "Feel me. This is what you do to me." Lawson pressed his erection to Dayne's buttcheeks. "Don't doubt that I want you. But I won't cause you more pain."

Dayne reached around and stroked Lawson's hips. "No one has touched me like this since the accident. It's been so long."

Lawson reached around to Dayne's belly, stroking him in long, slow movements from his chest to sliding along his cock.

Dayne wanted to be whole. "Please, Lawson." This was not the time for long explanations or reasoning. He flexed his hips, sliding his butt along Lawson's cock, telling him exactly what he wanted and needed.

He felt Lawson shift behind him and heard a drawer slide open and then shut again. A familiar snick, and Dayne sighed, then tensed a little as Lawson rubbed his butt, tapping his opening with a finger. It had been so long, and he groaned softly when Lawson broached him.

"Do you have any idea how hot you are?" Lawson crooned into his ear as Dayne quivered in Lawson's embrace. "You make me want you more than you know."

"Then take what you want." Dayne arched his back, pressing into the sensation. "I need to feel you."

"Are you sure?" Lawson sucked on his ear, and damn if Dayne didn't nearly come just from anticipation. He needed to feel the way he had before the accident.

Lawson stilled behind him, and then a rip, soft and unbelievably erotic, rent the air. Who could have thought the opening of a condom wrapper could send a thrill charging through him? Dayne waited, and then Lawson pressed to him. He relaxed his muscles as best he could, drawing Lawson inside him, making them one, Lawson filling him and sending his body and mind tumbling into passion in a way he didn't think he'd ever feel again.

"Oh, yes." He pushed back, Lawson's cock sliding deeper.

"Jesus...." Lawson growled as Dayne pressed to his hips. He wanted Lawson deep, and that was exactly what he had, stretching, filling, the two of them joined together.

Dayne felt Lawson's restraint as he held him gently, arms shaking. "You aren't going to hurt me. I'm not breakable." Dayne slammed back against Lawson to the deep rumble of Lawson's groans. Dayne wanted to see Lawson, but with his injuries, that position wasn't open to him. His legs wouldn't allow it, but being held tightly, with Lawson's warm breath on his neck, made up for it. He closed his eyes, holding his arms over Lawson's, stretching his neck so Lawson could kiss him.

"You make me feel so special," Lawson whispered into his ear.

Dayne didn't understand how that was possible, but he took what Lawson said as truth and hummed his happiness. His heart pounded, and he tightened his grip on Lawson's arm to keep from flying apart. Every part of him was on fire. "Oh God." Lawson switched angles slightly, and Dayne shook with uncontrollable desire. He felt alive, like the person he'd been before the accident, before his life had changed forever. It was temporary, but Dayne felt whole. He gripped Lawson as hard as he could, and Lawson groaned, gritting his teeth, hissing as he shook, trying to contain his energy.

Dayne didn't want Lawson to hold back. He wanted everything. Pushing back, he took what Lawson gave and dragged more out of him.

"You're—"

"I want you. Let it go and give me all of yourself."

Lawson slammed into him, and Dayne grunted and pressed his hips back. He needed more and felt Lawson's control wavering and then breaking. Lawson gripped Dayne's cock, stroking him as he snapped his hips, groaning as he finally let go. Dayne gasped for air as the power in Lawson washed over him, pushing Dayne to heights he'd never known were possible.

"Yes… God… yes."

"I've wanted you, but I was afraid…." Lawson's words came out between breaths and gasps. It was so heady to hear him reduced to moans and gasps—not that Dayne could say much more himself.

Sweat broke out on his forehead and on his back as the heat between them became too much to contain. Dayne was so close, and though he wanted this to last, it couldn't. Lawson was in complete control now, Dayne's pleasure in his hands. His hips met every thrust, emptying and filling while Lawson's hand slid along his cock, driving him wild because both sensations were so overwhelming on their own that he wasn't sure where to concentrate. Not that it mattered, because soon enough he teetered on the edge, and Lawson gripped him tighter, sending Dayne flying off into near oblivion.

For a few seconds, he had wings and no need of legs. He soared over the clouds before gliding back to earth and into Lawson's arms, where he belonged and hoped to stay.

LAWSON WAS still in bed, and Dayne hobbled out of the room early and as quietly as he could. When he'd called his doctor's office, they'd said they could get him in first thing in the morning. Dayne knew Lawson would want to go with him, but this was something he had to do alone. He went to his room, dressed, and then hobbled back to Lawson's room, kissed him good-bye, and left the house with all his books for class.

After a ten-minute drive, he parked and went inside the orthopedist's office, nervous as hell. He told the receptionist who he was and handed over his insurance information. He turned to sit down, but she instructed him to come right back, and once inside one of the little rooms, he waited for the doctor.

"Dayne," Dr. Olava said as he came in. "I understand you're having some pain."

"Yeah. Over the last few days, it's gotten worse, and I've been using the cane again." He lifted it for emphasis.

"All right. Can you get onto the examination table?"

It took Dayne longer than he liked, but he got up and lay down.

The doctor examined both legs, then spoke. "The left leg is doing very well. It seems strong, and you have some mobility in your knee that wasn't there the last time I saw you. But mobility in the right leg has decreased, and the muscles, while surprisingly strong, are doing what they can to make up for other weaknesses, and I think that's what's causing the pain."

"So what do you suggest?"

"I want to run some tests and take a closer look, but I'd like to go in and replace the knee. We've talked about this before, and while it will mean you'll have limited mobility with your one leg, we can immobilize it with a brace to prevent further injury while it heals, and with crutches you can get around."

"But will it do anything?"

"You could be largely pain-free and be able to use your leg more. There are always risks, especially with someone so young. The artificial knee will wear out and need to be replaced eventually. But it's my opinion that the benefits outweigh the risks. You're having trouble walking, and soon you'll be in even more pain as time passes." He helped Dayne sit up. "This is the best course."

"I just don't want any more surgery."

"I know, and I don't blame you. But I believe this will help."

Dayne hesitated. "If I were to go along with this, how would it work?"

"Part of the process will be to scan the knee so the joint can be made to your exact body size. The old way was to size them like shoes. Now we can make one that will specifically fit you. It reduces healing time greatly."

"How long will I need to be off my feet?"

"You'll need help for about two weeks. I know you're in college, so you can go to class, but you'll need to stay off your leg and let it heal. Do you have someone who can help you?"

"I don't know." Dayne didn't want to ask Lawson. He'd already done enough for him already. "I'll have to think about it." Since it was only one leg, he could use crutches to do what he needed to and take care of himself. He was going to have to find an apartment until he could figure out what to do as far as a house went. "This is all so much at once." He explained about living with a friend because of the fire.

Dr. Olava opened his computer and began typing. "I'm going to order some tests, and we'll get you in as soon as possible. Let's see what they show before we make a final decision," he said, and Dayne agreed, even though he was pretty sure the doctor was right. This had been coming on for a while, and he was going to have to face the reality of his situation.

After Dr. Olava wrote up the orders, Dayne worked with his office to schedule the appointments. It looked like he was going to be busy for the next few days. When he left, his head was spinning, but he needed to get to class.

A text came through from Lawson before he started the engine.

Are you okay? You left early.

I went to the doctor.

What did he say?

Dayne was trying to figure out what to tell him when his phone rang. It was Lawson. "They want me to have surgery to replace my knee."

"Is that what you expected?"

"No. I was really thinking it could have been worse. He thinks that will give me more mobility. But it means more appointments, tests, and then the surgery and weeks of recuperation." There was no way he was going to ask Lawson to take care of him. "And let's not forget more pain. I don't want more surgery, but I think it's the only option, so I'm going through with the tests, and we'll see what happens," he said, trying to make the best of it. "I'm on my way to class now, so I'll see you when I get home."

"I'm leaving for my jump, and I'll call you later."

Lawson ended the call, and Dayne's stomach twisted. He hated the thought of Lawson jumping out of an airplane, but it was something Lawson loved, and Dayne wasn't going to tell him not to do it. Instead, he pushed the worry out of his head and went on to the college.

CLASS DRAGGED on, not because the material was dull, but because Dayne kept glancing at his phone, hoping for a text message from Lawson. As his last class was letting out, his phone vibrated. It was Lawson saying he was on his way home. Dayne breathed a sigh of relief. He stopped by the library to get some research materials before driving back to Lawson's.

His phone vibrated again. *Just got called in to work.*

Dayne couldn't answer while driving, so he sent *Be safe* when he reached the house, then went inside. Tati greeted him, and Dayne used his cane to make it to the living room. He set his backpack on the sofa and sat down, breathing a sigh of relief as the pain in his leg lessened. He hadn't done much that day, but he was tired as hell and just sat still, stroking the cat. When he caught his breath, he pulled out his books and got to work.

He hoped Lawson wasn't going to be too late, but if he'd been called in, that meant a fire somewhere, probably a big one. He turned on the news, but he didn't see a story about a fire, so he turned it off again. Dayne sent Lawson a text to call when he got a chance, but didn't receive a reply. If Lawson was working, he wouldn't necessarily be able to contact him.

Dayne finished his reading assignments, as well as completing the various short-answer essay questions that went with the topics. Most of his instructors didn't assign them, but Dayne always reviewed them in order to make sure he fully understood what he'd read. By the time he was done, he was exhausted. He made a sandwich for dinner and lay down on the sofa, turned out the lights, and watched a movie with Tati lying on his chest.

Dayne fell asleep and woke hours later. The house was still quiet, and the movie was over. *Singin' in the Rain* was playing now, and he watched it for a few minutes before giving up and going to bed. He checked his phone but hadn't gotten a response from Lawson. He sent another message and ended up placing his phone next to the bed before climbing in.

Dinging invaded his dreams, and it took Dayne a while to realize it was his phone. He snatched it off the nightstand and answered it just in time. "Lawson?"

"It's Angus."

"Oh." His mind was still groggy, and he wasn't thinking clearly. "What is it? What's happened?" Suddenly he was awake and focused. If he was getting a call from Angus, then something had happened to Lawson.

"Lawson has been detained at a scene. The fire is out, and he's okay… physically. He asked me to call you so you wouldn't worry. But…." He sighed. "Look, he'd kill me for saying anything, but he's going to need your help. This wasn't an easy fire, and… I'm going to send him home as soon as I can."

"I'll be here." Dayne got out of bed, checking the clock. It was just after one. He put on some clothes and grabbed the throw from the foot of the bed. Dayne made his way downstairs to the living room, where he got comfortable on the sofa and waited for Lawson to come home.

He'd dozed off, when he heard the front door. Dayne hurried to his feet and met Lawson in the front hall. Lawson was pale and moved like an automaton.

"You didn't have to wait up." Lawson dropped his bag, not taking it to the basement the way he usually did. Instead, he shuffled into the kitchen and pulled a beer from the refrigerator, popped it open, and drank the whole thing before getting another.

"Lawson, what happened?" Dayne moved closer, but Lawson didn't acknowledge him or move, other than to drink probably half the second beer and kick the refrigerator door closed. Lawson turned toward him, setting the beer on the counter. He leaned over it without speaking. Dayne took him by the hand and led him out of the room. There was no fight in him; he simply followed where Dayne took him as though he were walking in his sleep. "Tell me what happened."

"I can't. I don't want to talk about it. I'll finish the beer and go to bed. I just need some time when things like this happen."

Dayne got Lawson to the sofa and half pushed him down on it. Asking again wasn't going to do anything, so he figured he'd wait him out. Damn his leg for hurting, though.

"I was called in for a business fire downtown, but it wasn't nearly as bad as they thought. So I was already there when we got a second call, this time for a house fire. It was bad—real bad. The mother was screaming that her children were inside. So I suited up and went in with another firefighter. We had just minutes to make it to the back bedrooms. I got there first and found both kids in their room, broke the window, and passed them outside before following. I radioed that I had them and heard the other officer say he was on his way out. Then the whole place came down around us. I barely got out, and I was racing away from the conflagration when I hear a scream and see the mother on the ground, rocking back and forth."

"Oh God…." Dayne knew what Lawson was going to tell him, but he held it together and sat next to him.

"The youngest child—he must have been two or three—wasn't breathing. His sister seemed to be okay, but the baby...." Lawson closed his eyes, and Dayne hugged him, slowly rocking Lawson.

"It wasn't your fault."

"I know. But it doesn't make me feel any better." Lawson's voice broke. "It's always this hard when it's a child. The mother fucking made it out, but she didn't think to get her kids. What kind of person does that?" Anger and resentment filled the room, rolling off Lawson in waves.

"Is that fair?"

"Nothing is fair. A young kid... a baby... died in a fire because I didn't reach him in time." Lawson's voice broke again. "If I could have gotten to him a little quicker, or if we'd arrived a little sooner, then I could have...." He stopped midsentence and grew quiet.

"It's not your fault, and you know it," Dayne said more firmly.

"I do. But it doesn't make me feel any better. This isn't the first time something like this has happened, and I'm sure it won't be the last."

"I know." He'd always known Lawson's job was dangerous, but he hadn't taken time to consider how bruising it could be to Lawson's heart. Every day Lawson helped people—it was what he did—and each time he went out, there was the chance that he could get hurt or help someone. But there was also the possibility that he wouldn't get there in time, like today. And what bothered Dayne was that he didn't know what to do for him. "Come on. Let's get you upstairs so you can clean up, and I'll make you some grilled cheese."

Lawson didn't move at first, and that was fine. Dayne liked holding Lawson for a change. Since they'd known each other, Lawson had been the strong one, and he'd done the comforting. Lawson had been a rock for him, and now Dayne got to return the favor.

Dayne turned away and sneezed once, then again, the stench of smoke and fire on Lawson's clothes overwhelming. Lawson slowly got to his feet, turned to leave, and stopped dead still. He just stood there as though he were trying to figure out what he was going to do.

Dayne carefully stood, took Lawson's arm, and led him out of the room and up the stairs to the bathroom. "Go ahead and get cleaned up. You'll feel better." Dayne started the shower, and Lawson began to undress. Dayne didn't want to leave him, so he undressed as well and got under the spray, helping Lawson inside. The water cascaded over both of them as Lawson held him tightly.

"It was so bad," Lawson whispered. "A little boy, three years old, I think."

"I'm sorry."

"I heard the mother crying and saw her daughter trying to comfort her and then crying as well." Lawson shook in his arms and then tightened his hug, shoulders bouncing as the emotion broke. Then he finally let go of what he'd been holding on to and started to cry. Dayne closed his eyes because he knew he was a huge blubberbox and was going to cry right along with Lawson. But he needed to be strong. That's what Lawson needed right now.

Dayne reached for the soap, lathered his hands, and began washing Lawson's chest, needing to do something normal. He ran his soapy hands over Lawson's shoulders and up his neck before reaching for the bar again and running it around his chest and down Lawson's belly. "Turn around," Dayne said softly, and Lawson listened. "Put your hands on the wall." Dayne kissed his shoulder, and Lawson complied like he didn't have a mind of his own. Dayne soaped his hands and washed Lawson's wide back, ran hands over his hips, and then soaped his hard, firm ass and down his tree-trunk legs.

He wrapped his arms around Lawson's waist and pressed to him, holding him, leaning his head on Lawson's shoulder. "Just let it go. I know what happened, and it wasn't your fault."

"But why?"

"That's always the big question, but there isn't an answer. Why did Jeff die in the accident? More than once I wished it had been me.

I wished he had lived and I could have been the one to go. But that isn't how it works. We get the chances we get, and that's all. I loved Jeff and still do, but I think I'm starting to see that I was spared so I could have a second chance at happiness." He let his hands roam over Lawson's chest. This wasn't the time for sexiness, but his body didn't seem to be listening. He tried not to pay attention, hoping his dick would go back to sleep, but when he let his hands glide lower, he encountered Lawson's cock, hard and thick and pointing toward the ceiling.

Dayne soaped his hands once again and slid them over Lawson's cock, stroking and petting him. "That's it. Just breathe and close your eyes," he crooned softly. Lawson leaned back, and Dayne twisted his hand slightly, teasing the flared head. Lawson quivered in his arms as Dayne continued stroking. He could feel Lawson coming apart next to him, the pain and pleasure mixing until neither was distinctive. Dayne knew the unusual pleasure that came from this kind of mixture. He'd experienced it after one of his multiple surgeries. "Just let it all go. I'm here and I've got you." He continued stroking as Lawson leaned forward, resting his head on the tile. "It's all right. Give yourself over to me. I won't let you fall, I promise." Dayne felt Lawson reaching the edge, and then he tumbled over quickly, crying out in pleasure that quickly devolved to tears.

Dayne held him as Lawson finally really let go. He gently guided Lawson back under the water and washed his hair as he stood docilely in his arms. Once the soap and shampoo were gone, Dayne turned off the water, grabbed Lawson's towel, and dried his skin before helping him out of the shower. "Go get into something comfortable, and I'll make you something to eat. Then we can go to bed." He hoped that the fatigue, both emotional and physical, would allow Lawson to sleep.

Once Lawson left, Dayne hung up the towels and went to dress before carefully going down the stairs to make some sandwiches.

"I'M SORRY," Lawson mumbled as he came into the kitchen, his hair still damp and plastered to his head. "I shouldn't have fallen to pieces like that." Lawson's cheeks blazed red, but Dayne ignored it as he set a plate on the counter in front of him. Then Dayne leaned against the counter across from him.

"You're human, and you reacted the way most people would, and…." He took Lawson's hand. "You have nothing to feel sorry for."

"I-I never…," Lawson stammered.

"You never go to pieces," Dayne finished for him. "You're always strong, and you handle things alone."

Lawson nodded.

"Is that what you really want, or just how you've been doing things?" Dayne cocked his head slightly. "You don't have to be strong all the time. I won't tell anyone or do anything to blemish your reputation."

Lawson picked up his sandwich and took a bite, still holding Dayne's hand. "You… I…. Being a gay fireman is hard. Sure, there's Angus and Morgan, but they're it in the department, as far as I know, and the other guys like to give us shit sometimes. If I showed any weakness, they'd pounce on it."

"I can see that. But this is your home, and I'm not a firefighter. I'm a crippled fire victim, and…."

Lawson squeezed his hand and pulled him closer. "I'll make a deal with you. I'll talk to you about shit if you stop with this cripple thing. You're stronger than you give yourself credit for." Lawson's eyes appeared watery.

"So are you." Dayne leaned over the counter, and Lawson stood, cradled his cheeks, and kissed him. "Sometimes it takes more strength to handle the emotional stuff than it does the physical." He kissed Lawson again. "Finish your sandwich, and we'll go to bed."

Lawson ate slowly, and Dayne took care of the dishes. His leg wasn't aching as much, and he figured he'd take something for the pain when he went back upstairs. Once Lawson had finished, Dayne put his glass and plate in the sink, and they went to Lawson's room.

Dayne got into Lawson's bed and waited for him. This was feeling as natural as breathing, and he curled up, warm and safe. Lawson joined him, slipping under the covers, and turned out the light. Dayne pushed up close to him and closed his eyes.

"You're just lying awake, aren't you?" Dayne asked after a while, feeling Lawson's nerves nearly shaking the bed.

"Maybe it would be best if you slept in the other room. I'm only going to keep you awake. My head isn't going to stop spinning no matter how much I want it to."

Dayne knew that was true, and he pushed back the covers, got out of the bed, and went back to his room. He saw the diary on the bedside table, picked it up, and took it back to Lawson's room.

"What are you doing?"

Dayne climbed back in the bed. "I thought I'd read to you."

"You have to go to class tomorrow."

"Not until the afternoon, so I can sleep in." He turned on the light. "Maybe it will take your mind off things."

"April 16, 1909

"My spirit soars today, and I know why I've been sent here. Sometimes the plans the spirits have for us are hidden deeply and take time to reveal themselves, and today that happened. I want to remember this day forever.

"It was warm and bright. The trees are still bare, but the sky was all white with cracks of blue showing through as Matthew and I walked through the woods. He took my hand and pulled me behind a large oak, pressed my back to the rough bark, and there he kissed me. Up till now the kisses have been tentative, almost fearful. Today it was warriorlike, Matthew taking what he wanted, and I did the same in return.

"He inflames me, and I want to hold him always. I asked him to return to my tribe with me when school ends at the start of summer. He didn't give me an answer right away, and I wasn't sure what that means. At least not until Matthew's smile lit his face and he kissed me again. Then Matthew told me he loved me in our own tongue, not that

of the White man. He said it with his heart, and I took his hand. The sun danced on his face, brightening as it broke through the clouds.

"Matthew kissed me again. The sun continued to brighten and warm the air around us until it was hard to breathe. Matthew guided me down to the forest floor, held me, and made me his, giving himself to me. He is in my heart, and I will forever hold him there. He is mine and I am his.

"The White man says that what we do is wrong. I know that. But I feel Matthew in my heart, and I cannot let go of him. He will be there forever. I have found a hiding place within my room, and I am keeping my diary there from now on. It will be safe. I must keep our hearts safe.

"We are warriors, and we will fight for what we have."

Dayne closed the diary and let it settle on his chest.

"Is that the end?" Lawson asked. "That seems like such a nice way to leave things. Too nice."

"That is the last entry in this volume." Dayne set the worn clothbound book on the nightstand and turned off the light.

"That's it?"

"For tonight. They're happy, and I think that's a nice place to leave it for now." Dayne sensed it wasn't going to last for them.

"Are you happy?" Lawson asked in the darkness.

Dayne was afraid to answer, because every time he allowed himself to be happy, it always fell apart. He moved closer to Lawson and pulled Lawson's arms around himself, pressing Lawson's big chest to Dayne's back. "Yes, I am." There, he'd said it—now heaven help them both.

Chapter 8

THE NEXT few days were quiet. Dayne went to class, and Lawson used his remaining time off to rest and try to get his head around what had happened with the child he'd lost in the fire. In the past, he'd simply buried his feelings and that had been that. But this particular incident didn't want to be buried, and he'd ultimately made an appointment with the department psychologist.

"How did it go with the doctor?" Dayne asked when he came in the house.

"I could ask you the same thing. What did the doctor say about your tests?"

"I asked first." Dayne set down his bag. He was moving more stiffly each morning, and though he loosened up during the day, Lawson could see he was hurting. Dayne sat next to him, and Lawson turned off the television.

"We talked about what happened, and he said the same thing you did. I know it wasn't my fault, but I can't help wondering." Lawson turned away. "He did say that part of what made me good at my job was that I took things to heart. Now, that's a whole bunch of—"

"No, it's not. He's right. You rush into those buildings because you want to help people. It is what makes you good at what you do. If you didn't care, you wouldn't do it."

Lawson shook his head. "That's what I tell everyone. But I think I get off on the adrenaline. There's no head rush as great as trying to outrun a fire, getting to the people before the flames do, and getting them out."

Dayne stared at him, openmouthed. "Is that what you really think? That it's a game?"

Lawson sighed. "Not a game. I don't understand it."

"Maybe you're feeling so badly because you know it isn't a game. You could get by telling yourself that, and now it doesn't hold water." Dayne patted his leg.

"But how do I go back to how things were?" Lawson didn't want to worry about this kind of thing. How could he do his job if he was worried about everyone he went after? "When I go into a building like that, I believe that I can do it. That I'll always get there in time to get the people out. I knew it in my heart. Even when I didn't, it was never this close before. If I could have gotten to that kid just a few minutes earlier, his little lungs would have had a chance. But I didn't—I was too slow. And what if I'm too slow the next time, or the time after that?" He probably wasn't saying it right.

"Everyone doubts themselves every now and again because none of us wins everything all the time, and you won't always get there. I'm sorry to say so, but it's true."

"Then what do I do?" Lawson asked.

"If I were in that position, I'd… well, I can't, but I'd want to ask my mother."

Lawson sighed and checked the time. Then he dialed his parents and left a voice mail when they didn't answer. "Mom and Dad will call me back when they can." The relationship he had with his parents had changed a lot since they'd moved to Florida. He still loved them and all, but they had their lives, which he mostly wasn't part of any longer.

"Do you miss them?"

"Don't change the subject." Lawson scooted closer on the sofa. "What happened at the doctor's?"

"They did the scans for my new knee the other day, and he said it all looked as he expected. He wants to schedule the surgery for a week from today. I'll miss a day of classes, but I can get the work to do ahead of time. He says I'll have the weekend to recover and will be on crutches for a while." Dayne turned to him. "I don't want more surgery. I keep wondering what will happen if something goes wrong. I came close to losing my legs before."

"But this could make you better, and you'd be in less pain."

"Maybe. But things can always go wrong, and what am I going to do for weeks afterward? I won't be able to get around very well. I was looking for apartments near the college, but they're all pretty full, and the ones I could find all had stairs."

"You'll stay here. This...." Lawson was about to say this was Dayne's home. It wasn't, even though his house felt more like a home with Dayne here. They'd never really talked about him staying, and since Dayne had been looking for a place, then maybe he wasn't as happy here as Lawson thought he was. "I have room for you."

"But I won't be a burden to you or anyone."

"You wouldn't be. I'd have to work, but I could be here to help you get down the stairs in the morning and then upstairs again at night. Tati would keep you company when I'm not around, and I know if you left, she'd miss you." He'd miss him too, but Lawson wasn't sure if his heart was rushing in too quickly or not. The thought of Dayne leaving made his stomach flutter, and he wanted to hold him tight and never let him go. But Dayne was an adult and had to make his own decisions.

"Let me think about it, but I won't put a strain on anyone. I've had my legs out of commission before, and I know how hard it can be. At least this time it's only one. But still, I won't do that to you. I can take care of myself."

"Yes, you can, but you don't have to. There's a difference." He realized he'd take care of Dayne and love him for as long as Dayne would let him.

"But why? You let me stay with you because you felt sorry for me after the fire, and now because I'm having surgery you want me to stay too. Do you have a thing for people once they're helpless? Do you need to be needed?"

Lawson was shocked and unable to speak at first, and when he did, his anger rose to the surface. "Are we back to that? And I didn't let you stay here because I felt sorry for you." He was on his feet almost before he could think about it. "You needed a place, and I offered one. That's all there is to it, and I'm offering you one now." He leaned closer. "Is it possible that I could like you and think you're a pretty incredible man? Does that even enter your mind?" Lawson rolled his eyes. "I know I'm not perfect, and if my last couple of boyfriends are any indication, I'm not very good at relationships. They left as soon as the thrill wore off."

"Excuse me?" Dayne grabbed Lawson's arm. "Here I thought you were giving me shit about my insecurities, and now… you have them too?"

"Of course I do. Guys think that I'm a fireman and want me to take them for a ride. I did plenty of that for a long time, and the few times I let a guy get close, he was gone." Lawson didn't move. "I'm not smart like you. I rush into buildings and fight fires. That's what I know and what I'm really good at. You're this brilliant man who has a huge future ahead of him. Nothing gets you down, and when it does, you start fighting your way back." Lawson looked down at himself and pulled off his shirt. "When guys look at me, they see this." He waved his hands in front of him. "That's all they see."

"When guys look at me, they see a limp and a cane."

"Not all of them." Lawson sat back down. "Some of us see the most incredible blue eyes the color of the sky in spring, and hair with so many highlights that sometimes when the sun shines on you, I swear you're on fire." He took Dayne's hand. "I first met you at the historical society, and I sat at your table. I didn't see your legs or your limp. At that moment, all I saw was you." Lawson looked deep into Dayne's now-watery blue eyes. "Your smile and the way you bit your lower lip just a little when you concentrated. The earnest way you approached your work, and the passion you had for what you were doing. It was in the way you sat and how you leaned forward whenever Beverly spoke with you. I didn't invite

135

you to stay here because I felt sorry for you. I invited you because I'd already seen you, the man you are, sitting in that reading room, watching me."

Dayne squeaked softly.

"I saw you looking, and I looked back." Lawson leaned toward Dayne, taking his chin in his hand, nearly closing the gap between them. "I'm not a fool, and I know what I want when I see it. Well, most of the time." He thought of all the time he'd wasted prowling around when what he'd really needed to do was step into a library to meet someone special. "I was trying to figure out how I was going to see you again, and there you were."

Dayne's lips moved but nothing came out. "Is that really how you feel?"

"Shit, yes, it's how I feel." Lawson stood and tugged Dayne to his feet. Then he put his phone in the dock and started some music. "I liked dancing with you." He gathered Dayne in his arms and shivered as Dayne ran his hands over his bare side and around to his back.

"But I can't dance."

"Sure you can. You're doing it now." Lawson swayed back and forth, barely moving his feet. He didn't want to cause Dayne any pain or discomfort. "Just lean on me to take some of the weight off your legs." He closed his eyes and breathed in Dayne's scent as the instrumental music continued. He didn't need much more to know he was falling in love with Dayne. And that scared him. Dayne had been hurt badly when he lost Jeff, and they'd never talked about things like that, so Lawson wasn't sure if Dayne was ready to move on. He thought he might be, but what if he wasn't? Could Lawson somehow compete with someone who was no longer around?

"What are you thinking about?" Dayne asked, looking up from Lawson's chest.

"Just you." He stroked Dayne's back and continued moving to the music. Lawson didn't get much quiet time in his life—he usually never stood still long enough to enjoy it. But with Dayne he was beginning to understand the lure of hours of peace with one special person: Dayne.

"We could go upstairs," Dayne offered.

"We will after dinner. Right now I want this." He gently swung Dayne around. "I don't know if I'm going to say this right, but I like the way you look at me."

"How is that?" Dayne smiled, and it was like the sun came out from behind a cloud.

"Like I'm the center of the world. I've had guys look at me with heated lust more times than I can count. And that only means one thing. You look at me with so much more."

"Because you are more than that. You have a kind heart that most people don't see." Dayne held him tighter, pressing his cheek to Lawson's chest once again. They danced together for a while, the songs changing but not the way they moved together. Song after song passed until Lawson gently danced Dayne back to the sofa. He guided him down and sat next to him, still holding his hands. Lawson continued swaying slowly to the music, dancing from the waist up.

"What are you doing?"

"Dance sitting—sit dancing? You don't have to be on your feet, and we can still dance all we want." He didn't miss a beat, and Dayne chuckled but continued moving with him. It was wonderful, and when the music ended, Lawson dipped him back onto the cushions, gliding the tips of his fingers over the slightly rough stubble on Dayne's cheeks. There was nothing sexier than that gentle roughness on his fingers.

"So what are you doing now?" Dayne asked, cocking his eyebrows slightly, placing his hands on Lawson's shoulders to stop him.

"Seducing you."

"Oh." Dayne gentled his touch and slid his hands around Lawson's neck. "Continue."

Lawson chuckled, and Dayne smiled before pulling Lawson down. "I intend to."

Their lips met in a kiss Lawson felt to his toes. It was earth-shattering and heart-mending all at the same time. This was what he'd been waiting for, looking for. But he hadn't known what he wanted. It was like going to dinner at a friend's house and discovering your new favorite food for the first time. Lawson could taste Dayne for the rest of his life and never tire of the sweet tang on his lips.

"What are you thinking?" Dayne said when Lawson hovered over him, peering into his eyes.

"That it's time we went upstairs. The bed will be so much more comfortable than the sofa." Lawson stood, grabbed his phone, and lifted Dayne.

"That's enough. I can walk." Dayne squirmed, and Lawson put him over his shoulders, patting his ass. "God, you've gone all caveman."

"You better believe it."

Dayne stopped squirming, and Lawson jumped as Dayne latched on to his asscheeks. "This is a great view." He kneaded Lawson's butt, laughing like a loon.

"Jesus." Lawson nearly dropped Dayne when he slid his hand inside his jeans and over his butt.

"This thing is like rocks. What do you do, squats for days?"

Lawson reached the bedroom, and Dayne stopped playing, patting his butt before Lawson laid him on the bed.

"If you're going to be a caveman, then I'm going to cop a feel, because that's way too good to pass up." Dayne grinned as Lawson tugged at his clothes. He needed more skin and much less coverings. Dayne helped and soon lay on the spread, naked as the day he was born and as beautiful as anything Lawson had ever seen. Dayne squirmed and tried to slide his legs under the covers. Lawson stopped him before kicking off his shoes, then stripping off the rest of his clothes.

"Don't hide." He lightly stroked up Dayne's legs before climbing on the bed. He kissed the scar just below Dayne's left knee and then upward. In some places the skin was mottled, and in others, crisscrossed with a network of fading pink scars.

"Why are you doing that?" Dayne shivered as Lawson glided his finger over the longest scar, which ran from his knee halfway down his leg. "It's really weird and sort of squicky."

"I want you to know that these are battle wounds."

Dayne sighed. "I was in an accident."

"Yes. But each scar is a fight back to where you are now. Therapy, pain, determination. They're all written here, and you need to stop trying to hide them." Lawson leaned forward and gently kissed the pink line. "Who made you feel this way? Was it one of those assholes from the club you told me about?"

"No. They weren't interested as soon as they saw me walk. They couldn't get away fast enough." He chewed his lower lip, and Lawson crawled up to where he could see into the depth of Dayne's eyes. "It was a guy about a year ago. Just after Mom died. He seemed interested enough, and we went out. The limp didn't seem like a big deal to him, and after a few dates, we went back to his place. The night ended with us getting in bed and him trying not to look at anything below my chest. When I rubbed my leg against his, he squirmed and made a face. Things were pretty much over for me, so I called an end to the evening and got out of there. As I got dressed, he made himself busy so he wouldn't have to look at me, and that was that. I learned what my legs looked like to other people."

"And you figured I and everyone else would act the same way? For a smart guy, you're kind of dumb. Not everyone is going to be like that." Lawson leaned in to nuzzle Dayne's neck, trying to rekindle some of the heat that had been there earlier but had dissipated when the conversation got heavier than Lawson intended. "You should be able to see that by now."

"I want to believe it. I really do." Dayne closed his eyes. "It's just that they're ugly."

"No, they're not. Your legs have scars. Okay, a lot of them, but they're as much a part of you as your belly button—which is cute, by the way." Lawson kissed above it, then tickled inside as Dayne chuckled at first and then groaned softly. "See, I know you like that."

139

Dayne's cock awakened again, stretching toward where Lawson was ministering, giving it a goal, and Lawson rewarded it by sucking the head between his lips and taking him deeper. Dayne whimpered and thrust his hips upward, quickly losing control, and that was exactly the reaction Lawson wanted. Dayne needed to let loose and feel free for a while. Lawson needed the same thing, and he was determined that both of them were going to have the experience of their lives. He ran his fingers along Dayne's perineum, teasing as he brought his finger closer to Dayne's opening before pulling away.

"God. Are you going to tease me all night or what?" Dayne's legs slid back and forth on the bed.

Lawson let Dayne slip from between his lips and stretched to reach the nightstand. He found what he was looking for, slicked his fingers, and teased his way back to where he'd been before sliding a finger home. The pressure and heat were amazing, pulsing and surrounding him. Dayne's whimpers turned to moans as Lawson sucked him deep once again.

Dayne tasted incredible, like salty bitterness, with the head of his cock sliding across Lawson's tongue. But the best part were the sounds—a symphony of moans and whimpers that went right from Lawson's ears to his cock, which bounced and throbbed as he ignored it to concentrate on Dayne. He was a firm believer in pleasing his partner to please himself, and that was especially true with Dayne.

Lawson bent his finger, sucking deep at the same time, and Dayne rewarded him with a half-strangled moan of surprise and hopefully delight. Lawson lifted his gaze, and damn, the sight was breathtaking. Dayne's mouth hung open, his eyes rolling, head rocking back and forth on the pillow, hands clenching the bedding.

"I'm going to…." Dayne gasped, quivering.

Lawson backed away to give Dayne a chance to breathe and reached for a condom. He put it on as Dayne rolled onto his side.

"I wish I could see you, but my legs…."

"Sweetheart, just being with you is enough." Lawson pressed close and slowly sank into Dayne's body. The heat was searing, the pressure around him eye-popping. He never wanted to hurt Dayne, so as much as instinct propelled him forward, he held back, taking his time, listening, stopping when Dayne patted his leg. Then he pressed forward again, Dayne moaning long and low until Lawson's hips reached his butt. There was nothing that compared to the way Dayne felt around him.

Lawson kissed Dayne's neck, holding him around the chest, stroking his belly and doing everything he could think of to connect with him. Usually during sex there was kissing and he could look into his partner's eyes, but this was what was comfortable for Dayne, and he didn't want him to feel like Lawson wasn't connected with him. "You're an amazing man," he whispered, sucking on Dayne's ear. He kept his motions slow and careful, letting Dayne set the pace, and Dayne met each movement with his own, holding Lawson's arms.

"You make me feel like I'm whole again."

"You are." Lawson kissed Dayne's shoulder. "You're amazingly perfect, and damn if I don't want you more than I've ever wanted anyone." He closed his eyes and nearly withdrew before sliding back into Dayne's heat. His head was already spinning, and with each thrust, the tingling and shaking that started in his feet rose and grew until he nearly lost it. He actually had to think unsexy thoughts for a few moments to keep any sort of control.

"Lawson!"

"I know, baby." He'd been angling for that certain spot and clearly he'd found it. Dayne came apart around him, and Lawson held him tighter as he shook through the throes of passion and then breathed deeply and held still. Lawson kissed him, loving the fact that he was able to make Dayne feel like that. He wasn't far behind, and with Dayne's heat around him, he climaxed seconds after Dayne, holding Dayne as tightly as he dared.

Lawson drifted for a while, listening to Dayne breathe and then stilling as their bodies separated. He didn't move until he had to, then took care of things and returned with a cloth to clean up Dayne before rejoining him in bed. "You know, we forgot to eat dinner."

Dayne laughed. "I knew there was a reason why I'm so hungry, but I don't want to get out of bed."

"Then stay here. I'll go order a pizza, and we can have dinner in bed and watch television if you want." Lawson grabbed his phone and placed an order for delivery. He got out his robe and laid it over the edge of the bed before joining Dayne under the covers, sliding next to him so Dayne could use him as a pillow.

It was so amazingly wonderful how easily they fit together. Lawson rarely lay around doing nothing, especially this early in the evening, but he could think of nothing better than this at the moment.

"Did you get a chance to skydive?"

"It was pretty amazing. There were some wild air currents that blew us first one way and then the other. Still I managed to land nearly dead center of the zone, which was awesome as hell. Skydiving isn't just about jumping out of the plane, but controlling the descent and landing on target."

Dayne shivered a little. "I know you're very good at what you do, but it still scares me. What happens if your chute doesn't open?"

"There is a reserve one that you trigger, and it will open. That's happened to me once. The primary chute got tangled and I had to cut it loose and open the reserve. It's something we practice and train for because, while it doesn't happen often, it can, and you have to be ready for everything. I check and recheck all my gear multiple times."

"I know you do." There was something in Dayne's voice. "I just wish you… I don't know. I have no right to say anything. You are who you are, and I need to accept that. You like to do exciting things, and I'd rather stay home and read." He shifted to look up at Lawson. "Are you sure you aren't going to get bored with me? Sometimes I think I get bored with myself."

"I don't think so." Lawson could honestly say he felt truly happy. "And when that happens, we'll just have to find exciting things you can do. Have you ever traveled?"

"No."

"Then we can do that. I love it. Can you imagine diving in the Caribbean to see the fish and coral? All those colors and amazing shapes lit by the sun dancing on the water above us. Or maybe we can go to Europe, take one of those river cruises and look at castles and have great food." He stroked Dayne's hair, loving the softness through his fingers.

Dayne yawned and then slowly got out of the bed.

"Where are you going?"

"I have some work I have to get done. I came home and got so excited to see you that…."

"After dinner," Lawson said, coaxing Dayne back into the bed. He heard a car out front, groaned, and went to get the pizza, knowing their quiet time was probably over, and that was okay. Dayne needed to keep up on the work for his classes, and just because he was falling in love with Dayne didn't mean the entire world came to a stop. Lawson put on his robe, watching Dayne leave the room, his tight little bare butt bouncing with each slow step.

"I'll meet you downstairs in a few," Dayne said, pulling him out of his daydream.

Lawson hurried down the stairs, met the delivery man, paid for the pizza, and placed it on the coffee table. He got a couple of beers and wondered how his plans for the evening had been shifted on their ear.

Dayne came in, carrying his bag, and set it on the floor next to the sofa. He settled and got a piece of pizza, then opened one of his books across his lap. This didn't seem promising, but then everything changed. Dayne squirmed, probably to get comfortable, and ended up leaning against him. Instantly he stopped moving, eating as he read. Lawson ate his pizza as well, turning on the television, volume low, one arm entwined with Dayne's.

They sat like that for hours. Lawson was afraid to move in case it broke the connection between them. Just sitting with Dayne made him happy. How in the hell had that happened?

"Listen to this." Dayne looked up from the book he was reading. "It's from Ted's second volume."

"April 28, 1909

"Mr. Marshall said today that all good things come to an end. I really hope that's not true. I spend my days thinking of Matthew and my nights dreaming of him, and he tells me he does the same. In class I watch him and see him watching me. No one else seems to notice and I know we must be careful, but I can't take my eyes off him.

"He is my world, the most important part about being here. I can endure the itchy clothes and boots that strangle my feet, the dirt, and the rules that make no sense, all for Matthew. Yesterday we went for a walk, and when no one was looking, Matthew took me into the trees. Spring is everywhere, and I can feel it racing through me, awakening joy and happiness I never knew was possible. As soon as we were out of sight of the school, Matthew and I raced through the trees, running at top speed. I felt like myself for the first time in months, and the spirits of the forest called to me, urging me to go faster, run farther. I never wanted to stop.

"Matthew hid and jumped out from behind a tree. He's playful, and his smile and laughter are enough to brighten the cloudiest day. We collided and rolled together on the bed of leaves on the ground. We laughed, smiling, his huge brown eyes suddenly piercing my soul. He touched me, deep inside without using his hands, and I couldn't move. Matthew's raven-black hair fell into his eyes, and for a second, I wondered how it had gotten so long without the school cutting it. But then he leaned closer and kissed me, hard, and I let him. I wanted this. I need to love him and be loved in return. Matthew gave my spirit wings, and he made me soar among the clouds.

"I want to be with Matthew always, and I asked him again to come home with me and be part of my tribe and family. I do not know if he will agree, but I had to ask him. Maybe that is where our good

thing comes to an end. I don't know. Like I said, I hope Mr. Marshall is wrong.

"I am a warrior and I will survive anything."

"Do you think he means what I think he means?" Lawson asked.

"That they made love? Yes." Dayne wiped his eyes with the back of his hand.

"Why are you shaking?" Lawson asked, gently putting his arms around Dayne's waist.

"Because I know that Mr. Marshall is right. All good things do come to an end. Somehow the bad and the hurtful always make an appearance." Dayne closed the book and set it on the sofa. "I'm scared to read any more because I know that the heartache is right around the corner for them. I want the two of them to be happy. After all they've been through, to find a small piece of happiness and…."

"You don't know what happened to them. What if Matthew went home with Ted and they lived quiet lives on the reservation for the rest of their lives?"

Dayne shook his head. "I'd like to hope so, but somehow I doubt it." He grew quiet. "I think I have all I need for my paper, at least from this diary. I need to return it to the historical society and get on with my other research. Let what I just read be Ted and Matthew's happy ending and leave well enough alone."

Chapter 9

DAYNE HAD been on edge for the last few days, and he had no idea why.

Things with Lawson were going well. He'd gotten a line on an apartment in Carlisle and made the mistake of asking Lawson to look at it with him. Lawson took one step in the apartment, smelled it, then walked around the living room and kitchen, checking everything out. He found the electrical box and looked that over before turning around and leading Dayne out.

"That place is a fire hazard." Within seconds they were back on the sidewalk, with the landlord completely flummoxed and Lawson telling him it wasn't the right place. "You should also have someone look at the electrical work before the building burns down." Lawson took Dayne by the hand, and Dayne found himself half propelled down the street.

"It wasn't that bad."

"It was awful." Lawson stopped and turned to him. "What's wrong with my house that you want to live in a dump like that?" He folded his arms over his chest, and Dayne's argument about not wanting to take advantage of Lawson died on his lips. There was nothing sexier, in Dayne's opinion, than a pissed-off Lawson, pushing his chest forward, eyes glaring like laser beams.

"Okay." There was nothing he could say, and Lawson had rather scrambled his thoughts to begin with.

"So you'll stop this apartment hunting and let yourself be happy?" It was a challenge if Dayne had ever heard one. "Because sometimes you can be a major pain in the ass."

Dayne giggled; he had to. "Look who's talking." If he hadn't already had a limp, Dayne would definitely be walking funny after Lawson's nightly, and getting more intense, lovemaking. He smirked, and Lawson puffed himself up even more, his lips curling upward in a proud sort of way. Damn, the man knew he was good. "If you let your head get any bigger, it isn't going to fit in the car."

"Besides, you've got your surgery coming up, and this isn't the time to be moving out on your own, and you know it."

"They postponed it," Dayne said.

"When?"

"They want to make a special knee for me, and it's taking more time than the surgeon originally expected, so they're going to do the surgery as soon as classes are over. So I thought I'd give you a break and…."

Lawson tugged him into his arms, right on the main street of Carlisle, with cars and trucks passing constantly. "If I needed a break, I'd say so. Just relax. I know what I want, and I told you I like having you in my house with me. It's where you belong." Lawson had said his piece, and then he gave the good people of Carlisle something to talk about for weeks as he kissed Dayne within an inch of his life, right near the busy square in the center of town. If anyone said anything, Dayne couldn't hear it over his heart pounding in his ears.

That had been Friday, and now Dayne was trying to get all his schoolwork done while the house was quiet. He hated the weekends when Lawson worked. When he had shifts during the week, Dayne was busy with school and following up on the ongoing insurance claim, which he'd been told was nearly complete. Thank goodness. That should have been very good news, but he was still nervous and jittery. Even Tati prowled the room, settling next to him and then moving on as though she had the feeling something wasn't quite right.

He messaged Lawson to say he missed him and was sitting with Tati. Lawson replied that he was with a bunch of guys who'd been working hard and smelled like it. Dayne put down his phone and went

147

back to his studies, finally letting go of his nerves and doing his best to relax.

His paper on the Indian school was coming along well. He had found a number of references to how the students were treated and the policies of the school, so he thought he had the angle he was going to take in his paper. After getting his other work done, he got started on outlining the paper. He had some very personal stories from journals and letters he'd found that detailed hardships the students had had to endure, specifically those related to the way the school attempted to remove them from their heritage and make them more "white."

Dayne got his computer and placed it on his lap. Tati tried to lie on it, but Dayne set her next to him and, using the outline he'd been building while doing his research, got started. These types of papers usually took him a long time to write, but this one seemed to flow. He had become invested in the plight of these young people, and he was passionate about the topic he'd chosen. That always made things so much easier.

He worked for a long time, stopping only to eat, and then returned to his work. He was deep in thought, typing as fast as his fingers would allow him, when his phone vibrated on the cushion next to him and Tati jumped straight into the air. She'd been sleeping on it, probably because it was warm.

Dayne glanced at the number and then answered it. "Hello?"

"Dayne, it's Richard." This was no social call; Richard's tone was instantly serious. "Morgan and Lawson got called to a fire."

Those words set Dayne on edge. He was already saving his file and setting his computer aside. "What happened?" He stood and carried his phone as his stomach clenched, adrenaline pumping.

"They were inside a home, trying to get the mother out, when the ceiling collapsed on top of them. Morgan apparently dove under the dining table, but Lawson only got partway under before he was hit. Morgan was able to get him out before the rest of the house collapsed."

Dayne reached for his keys but remembered they were on the table next to his bed, so he climbed the stairs to get them. "Okay." He tried to calm his nerves, and he grabbed his keys and returned to the stairs. "I take it he's on his way to the hospital."

"Yes. Morgan said he's being transported to Holy Spirit. He didn't tell me how badly he was hurt. No one is sure. Morgan did say that Lawson was alive, but that was all he knew."

Dayne started down the stairs, trying not to let his mind run rampant. He got about halfway down and grabbed for the railing as his vision began to spin. He must have missed, because the last thing he remembered was falling and crying out for Lawson, then blackness.

PAIN SHOT up his leg, and Dayne wished the world would stop shaking. He was afraid to open his eyes in case this wasn't some sort of dream and the entire world was indeed trying to shake him apart.

"You're awake," said a strange but comforting voice.

"Where am I?"

"It seems you fell down your stairs while you were on the phone with your friend Richard, and he called for help. I guess you have some real friends. He met us there and said he was going to lock up the house for you."

"Why does everything hurt?" Dayne took a glance at the woman sitting next to him and closed his eyes once again, trying to blot out the light, as well as the wail of the siren in his ears.

"Honey, near as we can tell, you hit your head very hard, which is why we have you on the board, and you hurt your leg pretty bad. I had to cut your pants and saw all the scars, so we're trying to take extra care of it. We should be at the hospital soon."

"Which one?" Dayne asked, his mind clicking on why he'd been so careless in the first place. "My boyfriend, Lawson, is a fireman, and he was injured at a fire today. I was trying to get out to go to him when I fell." At least that much he remembered.

"Holy Spirit."

149

"Thank goodness." All that Dayne could think was that if he was there, he could find a way to learn how Lawson was.

"You're worried about him."

"Yeah. I don't know how badly he was hurt. The other firefighter who got him out said he was alive and that's all he knew." Fear overrode the searing pain in his leg and the dizziness in his head. "You didn't bring him in, did you?"

"No, honey. I couldn't tell you anything about him if we did. There are all kinds of privacy laws. I suggest you ask about him when we get there." The ambulance made a turn and then pulled to a stop. The woman next to him stood as the doors opened.

Dayne knew what was coming next and braced himself. He closed his eyes, gritting his teeth, expecting the wave of pain that was to come, but they were so gentle that he barely felt a thing, and soon the lights brightened as he was wheeled inside to an examination room.

"You take care, and I hope you find out what happened to your boyfriend."

"Thank you."

Doctors and nurses surrounded him, shining lights in his eyes and then sending him down for X-rays without removing him from the board. Once he returned, Dayne was gently shifted to a table, his leg kept immobile.

He was afraid to move at all. At least his head was clearing, and he could think straight. They wanted him to lie still as they inserted an IV and then did their best to get him settled.

"Just lie here and the doctor will be in."

"Is there a fireman in here? Lawson? They said he was brought in. He's my boyfriend. I was trying to get here when I fell, and…." Dayne felt so stupid. He should have taken his time and made sure he got to the bottom of those stairs in one piece. Now he'd messed up his leg pretty badly, judging by the pain, and who knew what the consequences were going to be. He was here, but Lawson was God knew where, all alone, and what if…?

"I can't say."

"I know all that privacy stuff, but you should be able to tell me if he's here, because I'll find out if I have to hop around the entire emergency room on my good leg, dragging the IV behind me."

She sighed. "There was a fireman brought in, and he's still here. I can't tell you any more than that." She finished up what she was doing. "Try to get some rest. The doctor is probably going to order more tests and pictures to see exactly what's going on with your head and leg."

"My orthopedist is Dr. Olava. Please have him called. We were planning a knee replacement on the leg that I've messed up."

"I'll tell the doctors."

Dayne sighed and fumbled for the bedside phone, thankful his room had one. He wanted his leg treated by his own doctor. He called the orthopedist's office and explained what had happened and where he was. He was put on hold, but Dr. Olava came on the line less than five minutes later. Dayne explained what happened, and Dr. Olava said he was on his way in and would be in touch with the emergency room personnel. Dayne hung up, already tired, and his eyes drooped. They must have given him something for the pain, because his leg stopped feeling like it was on fire and fatigue settled in.

"We can't have you falling asleep until we are certain you don't have a concussion," the nice nurse said. "And we're going to take you down for some more tests."

"Whatever you need."

A man came in and began fussing with the bed while the nurse made sure everything was properly attached and prepared for movement.

His head was scanned, as well as his leg. More pictures were taken, and then he was returned to his small room and settled back in. While in transit both ways, Dayne watched to try to see if he could catch a glimpse of Lawson, but he had no such luck.

"What did you do?" Dr. Olava asked when he came in the room.

"I was rushing, and I think I must have missed a step or my leg gave out, I'm not sure, but I went down. My leg feels awful."

"I saw the pictures, and you're damn lucky you didn't break it. You did wrench your knee pretty badly, and as soon as we can get the swelling down, we're going to set up surgery to replace it. There isn't a better opportunity, and waiting is now out of the question."

"What about my head?"

"You're lucky you didn't crack it open. But despite you being out for a while, there aren't any obvious signs of concussion, which is damn near a miracle. So we're going to admit you for now, and we might send you home in the meantime, but if we can get the swelling down quickly enough, we'll just do the surgery."

"Okay." That wasn't ideal, but he was going to have to live with it. "One of the nurses said that my boyfriend was here. Is there any way I can see him?" Dayne knew no one could tell him anything, but he had to know how Lawson was doing.

"I'll see what I can do, but privacy laws prevent us from telling anyone but family anything. I understand the need for them, but a lot of the time, they have unintended consequences."

This was the most frustrating thing ever. "Thank you. I just want to know that he's okay." Dayne settled back on the bed. Cold packs were placed on his knee, and he did his best not to shiver because it only added to the discomfort. He was such a fool sometimes. All he kept thinking was, what if Lawson didn't make it? He'd be all alone. The doctor patted his arm and left the room.

Dayne wondered what he could do to somehow see Lawson. It was all he wanted. His leg and head didn't mean anything.

"Are you all right?" Morgan asked as he came in.

"What are you doing here? I figured you'd still be working."

"Lawson has me as his emergency contact, and Richard told me what happened, so I wanted to make sure you were okay."

"Where is Lawson?"

"Right next door."

"Is he awake?"

"No. The ceiling came down on him. He's got some burns, but it could have damaged his spine, and he hit his head hard."

Dayne closed his eyes to keep from crying. His throat burned and he couldn't talk.

"They're hoping that it's just swelling, and that once it goes down, he'll regain movement. There don't seem to be any broken bones, so that's good."

"But he isn't waking up."

"No, and they're trying to figure out why. His head was under the table with me, so his breathing device must have failed."

"Can I see him?" The divider between the rooms was clear, but there was a curtain pulled on Lawson's side. "I need to see him."

"Okay." Morgan stood and went to push the curtain aside.

Lawson lay on the bed. He was in some of his clothes and hooked to a number of monitors, IVs, and oxygen. Dayne wasn't sure if he could see Lawson's chest rise and fall at all. He was so still, and that freaked Dayne out most. Lawson was always so active.

After a few seconds, Morgan moved the curtain to its original position and returned.

"What can I do?"

"Just pray for him." Morgan choked up and turned away. "I called his mom and dad, and they're flying in as soon as they can. The doctor said they're going to move him to intensive care, and he'll be closely monitored. Like I said, they're hopeful but still looking for answers."

Dayne felt so helpless. "I guess." He turned toward where he knew Lawson was as nurses and doctors went in and out of Lawson's area.

"Is there anything you need?"

"They're going to keep me overnight, I guess, and possibly longer if they do surgery on my knee. Can someone bring me my schoolbooks?" He wasn't sure he was going to be able to concentrate, but he needed something to do. "There's a bag in the living room next to the sofa with everything in it, including my laptop. And please feed Tati."

"Sure. I'll get it, and Richard and I will bring it when we come back."

"Thank you." Dayne sighed softly. He should have known something would be around the corner. He'd actually dared to be happy, and now look what had happened. Not only was he laid up, but Lawson had nearly been killed, and who knew how bad things were going to be for him. Dayne's leg was one thing, but whatever curse sat on him had extended its reach to Lawson, and now he was paying the price. Dayne heard Lawson's voice in his head telling him he was being a fool, and that shit happens—deal with it—and Dayne groaned.

"It's going to be okay. Lawson is strong."

Dayne hung his head. "You can't know that. Yes, he's strong and brave, and damn it, I love him, but that doesn't mean he's going to pull out of this." Just when he might be willing to believe to the contrary, it seemed like Dayne could end up alone once again.

"I know, Dayne." Morgan sat in the chair next to the bed. "Lawson has been happy. You have to know that. These last few weeks, he's been like a different person. Lawson was always intense—rush in, get the job done, high energy. And he's still that, but now he laughs, and he isn't the first one to volunteer any longer."

"Have I been distracting him?" What if he was the reason Lawson got hurt in the first place?

"Yes. But I think in a good way. He's a great fireman, but before he was maybe a little reckless. Now there's more caution in him. And that's due to you, I think. He has something other than his job to live for." Morgan lightly patted Dayne's arm and stood. "I'm going to check on him."

"Yeah. I'll be fine." If Lawson woke up, Dayne didn't want him to be alone.

Morgan left the room, going around the divider to Lawson's side, and Dayne closed his eyes, trying not to let guilt take over. His mother always told him that guilt was mold and that adding it to anything

154

could turn it to crap, and she was right. He needed to concentrate on the here and now, even as overwhelming as it was.

The ER doctor came in. "I'm Dr. Marvello, and I've been looking over your results and speaking with Dr. Olava. We're going to admit you. He's working to get surgery scheduled to repair your knee, and if the swelling goes down like we expect, that could be as early as tomorrow afternoon. There are some papers you need to sign for us, and then we'll get you moved upstairs."

"Is Lawson going to be moved soon? His friend Morgan told me how he was doing."

"I can't discuss his condition, but I'll make sure his friend is kept updated, and he can tell you whatever he feels is necessary." He sighed, explaining as though it were rote, and it probably was.

"Okay. Thanks."

"We've already alerted upstairs, and they're getting a bed ready for you. It shouldn't be very long."

"I appreciate all your help."

Dr. Marvello shook Dayne's hand, and then he left the room.

Dayne lay back, closing his eyes once again. He tried like hell not to think of the bad things, but they seemed to come unbidden. He needed Lawson to be okay and wake up so he could tell him how he felt. Dayne should have done that before now, but he hadn't been really sure until the thought of losing Lawson centered in his mind, and now it was taking root. There wasn't much he could do now but wait and hope for good news so he'd get the chance.

"THEY'VE MOVED Lawson into intensive care and are tending his burns. They're still hopeful that the swelling in his spine will abate, but he isn't waking up." Morgan put Dayne's bookbag on the side of the bed and sat in the chair as Richard silently rolled up to Dayne's bed. He wished he could give his friend a hug. Dayne needed one himself right about now.

"You scared the shit out of me." Richard took his hand.

"I know. I was rushing to get back down the stairs and out of the house. I'm usually so careful, and I completely forgot about anything other than Lawson, and look what happened. I think I might have gotten dizzy or something—it's hard to remember."

"Do you know if they're doing surgery on your leg?"

"Probably." Dayne sighed. "Yeah." He removed the ice pack and set it aside, watching the clock. He was supposed to leave it on for ten minutes and then take it off for the same amount of time. "All I really want is to see Lawson. They took off my IV, thank goodness. That was driving me crazy, and the beep machines are gone. Now it's just a matter of making sure I don't start tossing my cookies and the swelling goes down in my knee."

"Smartass."

"At least my head isn't swelling." Dayne had been watching the news, but the politics that dominated it gave him a headache, so he'd turned the dang thing off.

"True."

Dayne opened his bag and looked through it, relieved to have his things. He hated missing classes, but at least he could keep up on the reading and other assignments. "I really appreciate you bringing this for me." It was going to be difficult keeping up, but he was going to do his best. Dayne hated getting behind, so being laid up like this was very frustrating and worrying. He didn't want to miss anything.

There was no Internet service, but he had used his phone to send messages to his professors to let them know what had happened and why he was absent. The last thing Dayne wanted was for them to think he didn't care.

"Have they said anything about why Lawson isn't waking?"

"No. Other than sometimes after trauma, the body and mind retreat. They're hoping he'll find his way back to us soon. The brain is unpredictable sometimes, and it's possible he was hit and I didn't see it, but they said they didn't find any injuries. We can only wait and see."

"That sucks." Dayne shifted. "I wonder if they'd be able to get me into a wheelchair. I'd like to visit him. I don't have anything that can infect him or anything, it's just my leg, and I'd like to see him before I go in for surgery. There are things I need to tell him." Dayne didn't think there was anything that could be done, and drifted to other topics, even though Lawson stayed close in his mind.

"I'm going to go check on him, and I'll call you if there's any change at all," Morgan promised, then leaned down to share a kiss with Richard before leaving the room.

"He's always like that, isn't he?"

Richard watched Morgan leave and then turned back to Dayne. "Pretty much. Things are so much better for us now. I was pretty messed up when he and I met again, and just like you, it was at a fire. I think you know that."

Dayne did and he nodded.

"The thing is, I'd been through a lot and was trying to deal with my PTSD on my own, and I was pretty much a basket case until I got some real help." Richard glided closer to the bed. "I think you may have some of what I had."

"Huh? I've never been in combat."

"Sure you have." Richard looked down at his immobile leg as Dayne put the ice pack on his knee again. "You went through one hell of an accident, then your mom passed, now your house has burned down, and you're worried about Lawson, as well as laid up again partially because of the aftereffects of the accident."

"Shit. When you say it all at once, it makes my life seem like a disaster area."

"No. It's just things that have happened. I had a bunch of them all at once too, and it makes each one harder to deal with. Even small things started to bother me."

"So what are you saying?"

"Talk to someone who understands and get what you're feeling out in the open."

157

"You mean the things like how I feel responsible for what happened to Lawson? Like if he weren't with me, he wouldn't have been distracted, and my bad luck wouldn't have rubbed off on him?"

"Yeah. Something like that." Richard rolled his eyes. "You heard how you sounded."

"Like some great big whiner who should be put out of all of our misery."

"No. Life is the way it is, and we only get one. Some of it's really good, and some of it's crappy. You can't let the crappy stuff ruin your life. Yes, the fire at your house sucked big-time, but you got Lawson out of it."

"Yeah. But what if…?" His lower lip trembled, and damned if he didn't do his best to stop.

"This is what they told me. Face your problems head-on. So let's say something really bad happens to Lawson. It isn't going to—he's going to be fine. But let's say something does. Would you give up having met him and knowing him for the time you did?"

Dayne didn't have to think. The answer was on the tip of his tongue. "No. He made me happy, and I hope I did the same for him."

"You did." Richard held Dayne's hand in his calloused one. "Don't doubt that. And do you really think that Lawson would somehow blame you for what happened?" Richard raised his eyebrows as though the idea was ludicrous. "So let go. Shit happens and we deal with it."

"Is that a Marine saying or something?"

"Nope." Richard leaned closer. "Man up before I beat the shit out of you. That's much more Marine."

Morgan came in the room with a nurse and a wheelchair. "She's going to hold the chair and adjust it, and I'm going to lift you into it."

The nurse adjusted the leg support, and then Morgan bent over the bed and lifted Dayne, with the nurse supporting his leg. Dayne got a bit of a shock when his ass hit the cool air, but he said nothing, and once sitting, he adjusted the gown so it covered his butt, and the nurse set the cold pack aside and covered him with a blanket.

"You can't stay long," she admonished, and Morgan promised they wouldn't before slowly pushing him out of the room.

"I'll wait here for you," Richard said, and Dayne heard the awful television click on.

"Before we go, will you grab the small brown book out of my bag?" Dayne had intended to return the journals, but he hadn't been able to. Morgan locked the chair, left, and returned within a minute, carrying the journal. He handed it to Dayne, who cradled it to his chest, and then Morgan slowly pushed him toward the elevator.

"How did you make this happen?" Dayne asked when the elevator doors closed.

"The supervising nurse, Laverne, she used to be in Emergency when I met her years ago. She owed me a favor. She also called down to ICU and told her daughter that we were coming." He pushed the button to go down. "You know how we arrive first for every call? Well, Laverne's grandson, Tyrell, is two, and my company arrived just in time to help Claudine give birth to him. By the time the ambulance arrived, she was holding her son and I was covered in... we don't need to go there. Just say that I was their hero and they haven't forgotten."

The elevator doors slid open, and Morgan pushed him down a hall to where a set of double doors opened for them. "Is this him?" asked a smiling woman with the highest cheekbones and most stunning near-black eyes Dayne had ever seen.

"Yes."

"This way. You have to be very quiet." She led the way into an area of near silence with small rooms around a central desk. Dayne saw Lawson lying on a bed with tubes and machines all around. He gasped as Morgan pushed him closer and then negotiated him until he was right next to Lawson's bed.

"If I take his hand, can he feel me?" Dayne asked Claudine.

"Honey, I like to think so."

Dayne took Lawson's hand and stroked the back and the palm. "What were you doing? I know you were trying to help everyone, but

159

you need to come back to me now." Dayne closed his eyes as they filled with tears. He leaned forward to rest his head on the bed next to Lawson.

"How long have they known each other?" Claudine asked from behind him.

"A few weeks, but look at them," Morgan answered quietly. "You have to know Lawson. He's brash and runs into everything he does, but he took one look at Dayne and that seems to have been it. I've never seen him happier. And then this...."

"It's good to see people in love." Claudine approached the bed, and Dayne kept his head where it was, as close to Lawson's heart as he could get. She checked Lawson over. "I can only give you another fifteen minutes or so."

"Thanks," Dayne whispered, lifting his head slightly, looking at Lawson. "You need to come back to me. I have so much I want to say to you. I was going to tell you how I feel, but I can't do that with you like this. So you need to wake up and look at me so I can be good to you." He sat up and wiped his eyes. "Just wake up, you pain-in-the-butt drama queen." He gasped and breathed evenly to keep his emotions under control. "I don't know what else to say to you. Tati is probably home having a fit that you're not there. I know she misses you." He squeezed Lawson's hand once again.

Dayne let go of Lawson's hand and opened the journal. "I know I told you that I was going to return these because they were happy and that's how I wanted things to end, but sometimes I have a hard time letting things go. The last entry we read was from the end of April."

"*May 7, 1909*

"*Last night after everyone was in bed, Matthew came to me and we snuck out to our special place. We've gone there many times, and last night Matthew told me again that he loved me and then he showed me just how much he cared for me. The spirits surrounded us, and I felt their approval and even their care around us, protecting both*

Matthew and me. It was as though they wanted us to be together and were standing guard over us.

"I asked Matthew to come home with me to stay. My tribe will shelter and protect us from the White man's laws. We will be cared for and accepted. He will be safe, and the two of us will be able to lead a life together. Matthew said that was what he wanted and would tell his family what he'd decided. Matthew chose me. The spirits were happy, and so was Matthew."

Dayne couldn't help smiling and continued.

"But now, in the light of day where spirits can't hide, everything has changed."

Dayne paused and lifted his gaze, wondering if this was something he should really be reading to Lawson right now. But he'd started and would finish.

"Matthew is leaving. He got a message this afternoon from his family that his father and older brother are very ill and that they need him to come home so he can help provide for his mother, brothers, and sister. He can't come home with me. I offered to go with him, but he explained that his people didn't believe what my people did. They would treat him as a woman, and he didn't want that. He said he was going to catch a train in two days and the headmaster was going to help him get back home. I don't know how he's going to do that. But after Matthew said what he was doing, I felt my heart shatter into pieces.

"I am a warrior, and I know I have to be brave and not show anyone what I am feeling or they will know I care for him, and I must keep those feelings between me and the spirits. They can know, but no one else. So I must be strong as my love leaves to go home, putting many miles between us. I don't know if I will ever see him again, but I will carry Matthew in my heart always.

"I am a warrior. I will be brave."

Dayne wiped his eyes once again and heard a sniff from behind him. He turned in time to see Claudine leave the room. "There's only one more entry in the journal. It's two days later."

"May 11, 1909

"The wagon to the train station left at eight o'clock this morning, carrying Matthew away from me forever. I didn't have the courage to go down to say good-bye in person. Instead, I watched from my window as Matthew left the main building, carrying the same bag he arrived with. He looked different dressed in his own clothes. Last night I gave Matthew the moccasins I'd made for myself months ago, and I saw he was wearing them.

"Matthew looked around, and I know he saw me because his expression changed and hints of the pleasure we gave each other appeared on his face. I know Matthew loves me, and I love him and I will always carry him in my heart, even if I never get to see him again. Then Matthew climbed on the cart, and the driver started forward. He grew smaller and got farther away with each passing second. I stood in place until I could no longer see him and then closed the window and turned away. There was nothing I could do. He is gone and I am alone here once more.

"It's almost too much to take. But I am a warrior and I am strong. I will survive and fight again."

He closed the book and set it on his lap, looking up at Lawson, hoping for some sort of reaction. In the movies it was times like this when people wake up, but of course nothing of the sort happened. Lawson lay still, and Dayne sighed softly before wiping his eyes.

"We need to get you back to your room," Morgan said softly from behind him.

Dayne sniffled and nodded, then kissed Lawson's hand and set it gently on the bed. He softly said good-bye to Lawson, and then Morgan slowly backed him out and took him to his room. Morgan

162

lifted him out of the chair and laid him on the bed. "Thank you." Dayne wasn't in the mood to talk at all.

"Richard and I will be back to see you this evening." Morgan squeezed his hand, and Richard glided up to the bed.

"Remember what I said, and be strong." Richard squeezed his hand as well.

"I'll try" was all Dayne managed to say.

Richard and Morgan left, and Dayne put the cold pack on his knee before turning away from the door and letting the tears finally fall. Lawson felt as far away from him as Matthew must have felt from Ted as he was leaving. The worst part was, the longer Lawson stayed away and didn't come back, the less the chances were that he'd be able to.

What if Lawson was lost to him forever? Dayne wasn't sure how he'd deal with that.

DAYNE WOKE in recovery the following afternoon, and his first thoughts were of Lawson and how he was doing.

The hospital staff had been to work early to prep him for surgery. Morgan had been in last night and told him that the swelling in Lawson's spine had lessened and that the doctors were hopeful no permanent damage had been done. Now they needed Lawson to wake up, something he hadn't done yet. This morning Dayne had been occupied with surgery and hadn't received any news.

"Dr. Olava said the surgery went very well," the nurse told him.

Dayne thanked her and answered her questions about his pain levels, all while wondering about Lawson. "When will I be able to go back to my room?" Someone must have known how Lawson was doing, and Dayne needed to make calls to find out. He had to know. His own condition was less important than Lawson's.

"In an hour or so." She helped him drink a little, and he lay back, closing his eyes.

"My boyfriend is here in the hospital, and he's been in a coma, and I'm concerned about him. I know you can't tell me anything, but I need to know how he is."

"Just relax and let the anesthetic wear off." She helped him with another drink, and Dayne swallowed hard. He tried not to worry, and once he was more awake, they transferred him back to his room, where he watched television and dozed to pass the time until he called Morgan, who told him he'd heard nothing more.

As time went on, the pain in his legs ebbed and flowed. Ice was applied to keep the swelling down, and he waited some more. Toward the end of the day, Dr. Olava came in to check his incision.

"It went remarkably well, given the extra damage that was done. The new joint went in easily, but we had to do some cleanup of scar tissue, so healing is going to be slower than usual. We'll get you on your feet soon, and I have someone coming in to explain the care, as well as talk you through putting the brace on and taking it off. They'll also work with you on crutches."

"When can I leave?"

"Probably tomorrow. Until then, take it easy and try to relax."

"I'll do my best." It sucked knowing he was in the same building as Lawson. So near and yet so far. All he wanted was to see him again, maybe to plead with him one more time to come back to him. "It isn't easy. I want to be able to see my boyfriend, but he's up in intensive care, and I'm here."

Dr. Olava looked at his watch, turned, and left the room. Dayne closed his eyes, figuring he might as well try to take his mind off everything, but Dr. Olava came in with a wheelchair and an orderly. "I'll take you down. It's in my patient's best interest to be in the best mental state possible."

"Thank you." Dayne pushed back the covers and was helped into the chair, leg supported, and then the orderly pushed him down the hall. They retraced the route he'd taken with Morgan, and they entered ICU with Dr. Olava clearing the way.

"Lawson," Dayne said when he entered the small room. He was shocked into speechlessness when Lawson turned his head, opening his big beautiful eyes when Dayne said his name. "You're awake."

"Yeah."

"When did that happen? You've been out of it for two days."

"I guess a little while ago. I was wondering where you were." He extended his hand, and Dayne moved in as close as he could and took it.

"I fell down the stairs at your house as I was trying to get here, so I've been dealing with my own mess." He turned and introduced his doctor. "Dr. Olava, this is Lawson." He couldn't help smiling. "They said you had swelling in your spine that might keep you from moving."

"I can feel my legs and have been moving my feet." Lawson demonstrated, and Dayne thanked all that was good in the world. Lawson was going to be okay.

"Were you burned?" Dayne leaned in, needing to touch him and to be close to him as much as possible.

"A little. I remember the roof beams coming down on me and then hitting my head on the table. But I don't know anything else or remember someone getting me out."

"Morgan did, and he's been here with you and me for the last two days." Dayne brought Lawson's fingers to his lips and lightly kissed them. "I thought I'd done this to you, that my bad luck had rubbed off on you and that this was the payback from the universe for being happy."

"Sweetheart," Lawson groaned gently. "This just happened because it happened. It had nothing to do with you. The house wasn't built well and was a death trap to begin with and came down around us. You aren't bad luck or anything of the kind."

"Yeah, but...." Dayne leaned forward, and Lawson gently stroked his head.

"There's nothing else to it." Lawson lay still as Dayne cried softly in relief.

"I came to see you yesterday, and you didn't wake up. I thought I was going to lose you, and I can't lose any more people I love." He lifted his head and tears ran down his cheeks. "Everyone I loved is gone—Jeff, my mom—and I thought I was going to lose you too."

"No such luck. I'm stronger than that, and there isn't much that can get me down." Lawson was growing hoarse, and Dayne quieted and just sat next to him, letting relief wash over him.

"I love you," Dayne said. "That's what I came down here yesterday to say. We weren't sure what was going to happen, and I had to say that to you, and now…." He hated being this weepy, but he couldn't help it.

"Were you reading to me while I was out?" Lawson asked groggily.

"Yes. I read from the journal. I wanted to try to remind you of something we did together. I was trying to reach you, and it was probably pretty lame…. Wait…. You heard me?"

"Yes. I heard voices and dreamed of you. Or at least I saw you. I couldn't hear what you were saying exactly, but I knew you were here. I tried to reach you, but you stayed just far enough away that I could never find you." Lawson looked like he was wearing out.

"I was right here, and now you're here with me." Dayne held Lawson's hand as he closed his eyes.

"He's asleep now, and that's probably best for him," Dr. Olava said. "Let me get you back to your room. He'll probably improve rather quickly now."

"I hope so." Dayne let Dr. Olava direct him away, then down the corridor, back the way they'd come. "Thank you so much for doing this. It meant the world to me." He could breathe easily for the first time in days, and when he got back to the room, he had the dinner that was waiting for him and went to sleep.

Chapter 10

ALL LAWSON wanted was to go home. Instead, he was still in a hospital bed, but raring to go. If he had to lie on his back for another day, he was going to go completely stir-crazy.

Dayne had been up to see him briefly, but getting around was difficult for him, and he wasn't able to drive, so he had to rely on others. Lawson had seen the pain in Dayne's eyes and the way he'd sat very carefully. Though he didn't complain for a second, Lawson knew.

A nurse strode into his room with her computer on a wheeled stand. "I need to check you out and then get you on your feet."

"Okay."

Of course, that meant taking more blood. He already felt like a damn pincushion. She checked him over and took his temperature and blood pressure before helping him out of bed. Dayne had done him the biggest favor and had brought him some T-shirts, light sweatpants, and underwear, so at least he could dress like a normal person rather than wearing those awful ventilated hospital gowns.

He slid to the edge of the bed, and she helped him up, then gave him a chance to make sure he didn't get dizzy.

"Just take it easy and let's walk down the hall. Often after incidents like yours, we need to take things one step at a time, and with spinal issues, there can be a recurrence, so just go slow."

He agreed but walked normally, feeling stronger almost by the hour. He made it all the way down the hall and wanted to keep going to the elevator and then out of the building, but he turned and went back to his room. "It feels great to be up."

"No dizziness or weakness in your legs?"

"No."

"The doctor has you scheduled for one last scan to see that everything looks good. He also wants to check your lung capacity because of the smoke."

Lawson lay back down and sighed. "Just get it over with so I can go home. I know I can't go back to work for a while, but at least I can return to my life." Lawson was sick of lying still, but did it anyway.

She just smiled and typed in her computer. "The doctor will be in later to talk with you. And I think you have a visitor."

Dayne propelled himself into the room on his crutches and sat in the chair next to the bed. "God, it's good to be here. Kevin brought me, and he said he'll pick me up in a couple of hours." He looked around. "Are your mom and dad still in town?"

"They went back to their hotel a few hours ago to get some rest. Mom and Dad have been here for hours, and they were getting worn out. They'll be back in a little while."

"It was nice meeting them, though I wish it were under better circumstances." Dayne moved closer to the bed.

"I thought you were going to return those." Lawson motioned to the journal on Dayne's lap.

"I was, but so much happened, and then Morgan brought them up to me when I was here, and I read you some of it while you were out. It's what you said you heard. I thought I'd read you now what I read to you then because it's important." Dayne got close enough that he was able to reach him for a kiss.

A throat cleared, but Lawson didn't pull away. It was time his mother and father got used to Dayne being in his life.

"You remember my boyfriend, Dayne." He nodded as his mother forced a smile.

"Yes, of course." She pulled a tissue out of her leather Coach purse and dabbed her eyes. "For some reason my allergies have kicked in." She put the tissue away and took Dayne's hand. "It's good to see you again, and doing so much better."

Dayne shook hands with Lawson's father as well. Both his parents seemed to have grown younger since moving to Florida. They seemed vital and were tanned and toned. His father's hair was completely gray, but his mother's was black, styled beautifully, her skin radiant. She looked amazing and every bit her Native American heritage, better than he could remember from when they lived here.

"It's nice to know that Lawson has someone. We've been worried about him being alone so much." Okay, maybe it wasn't what Lawson had thought it was. "I wish our meeting was under better circumstances, but I'm glad you're both doing so well." She sat in the other close chair, and Lawson's father took the one near the television.

"Mom, you know I've been trying to find anything on your great-uncle, the one who went to the Indian School. Dayne has been doing research on the school as well, but up until now, we haven't found anything."

"That's what I wanted to share with you," Dayne interjected. He opened the journal and read Lawson the last entry once again, barely making it through the part where Ted watched Matthew leave.

"Is that the last entry in the journal?" Lawson used the corner of the bedding to wipe his eyes. "It's so sad."

"Yes." Dayne nodded. "I was going to return the journals and finish my paper, but I went through the rest of the pages and found a single entry two pages later. It's undated."

"I miss Matthew more and more each day. It's like the light has gone out of my life. I know now what I had and what I lost.

"I, Flying Raven, love Soaring Eagle with all of my heart and always will."

Both Lawson and his mother gasped at the same time.

"Matthew is your great-great-uncle, the man you've been looking for. We've been reading his story all along. I only wish it had a happier ending."

Lawson raised the back of his bed. "Did I tell you why I was looking for Soaring Eagle?" He squeezed Dayne's hand, nearly unable to catch his breath. "I always thought Soaring Eagle was gay. He lived with another man the rest of his life." Lawson looked at his mother for confirmation.

"They were roommates," she said, but Lawson shook his head. "At least that's what my mother always told me. He and Flying…." She stopped. "Flying Raven." She gently reached out, and Dayne handed her the journal.

Lawson turned to Dayne. "As far as the family stories went— and they weren't talked about much—they spent their entire lives together. Details are sketchy, but my great-grandmother used to say to me that her brothers Soaring Eagle and Flying Raven proved that sometimes predator and prey could exist together. I didn't know what she meant at the time and thought it strange. But my ancestors believed that names had power. So she was saying that she knew they were lovers, partners."

"It sounds like that to me. And they did find each other again, just like you found your way back to me." Dayne rested his head on the bed, and Lawson gently stroked his hair. "I almost lost you."

Lawson watched as his parents exchanged looks and then quietly stood and left the room. "Hey. Don't get upset. I'm fine now, and I'm going home soon, and then…."

"I'll start looking for apartments so you can have your house back."

"I don't want my house back. It was too big and too lonely. I want you to stay with me. That is, if you'd like." Lawson bit his lower lip. He hated being nervous, but this was important. "I know what I want."

"Are you sure?"

"Yes. I need you, in my house and in my life." He'd been out of it for days, but now that he was awake, he knew what was important to him. Lawson continued stroking Dayne's hair until he lifted his head, and his eyes, shining with unshed tears, met Lawson's. "I need to settle down, and the doctors say that things like skydiving are probably out of my future."

"What about your job?"

"Well, instead of being the guy who runs in the burning buildings, I'll be one of the men who mans the hoses. The other guys always thought I took too many chances, and maybe they were right. But I never had anyone to be cautious for. Now I have someone I want to live a long life with—happy, hale, and whole." Lawson held Dayne close. "For a while, we're going to be two invalids who are going to need to help each other get through the days."

"I think I'm going to like helping you." Dayne smiled and raked his gaze down Lawson. "There are so many things I can help you with."

"Jesus." Lawson smiled, grateful his parents were out of the room.

"He's not going to help you." Dayne chuckled, and Lawson held him as closely as he could. "You know, I'm happy. Really happy, and that's when things usually got to hell."

"Then we'll face it together, whatever comes." He'd gladly face down a pack of wolves and anything else life could throw at him to be with Dayne. "I can promise you that."

"As long as you know what you're getting yourself into."

Lawson gently cradled Dayne's chin in his hand. "I do." Then he leaned closer and kissed him.

Epilogue

The Following Spring

DAYNE WAS done with classes for the school year and had just finished his last exam. One more year and he'd have his degree, and then he planned to teach, although he was still looking at alternatives. The best part was that he'd been offered a full scholarship at Dickinson for the following year. He was so excited that he could barely stop wriggling in the driver's seat on the way home.

"All done?" Lawson asked from the front door as Dayne walked up the steps without a cane and relatively pain-free. Now that his right leg felt good, the pain in his left leg, which had been masked, had come forward, but it wasn't nearly as bad, and Dayne was done with surgery for a while.

"Yes." He wasn't going to be running any marathons, but he climbed the front steps with ease.

"I thought we'd go out to celebrate, but first you need to put your things inside. I have a surprise for you."

Dayne put his bag inside the door and closed it again before locking it. "Okay, I'm ready." He hurried down the walk and into Lawson's arms. "Is this the surprise? Because if it is, we shouldn't stay out here."

"If we do, we'll frighten the neighbors."

"Hell." Dayne looked across the street. "The neighbors will be envious."

Lawson chuckled. "What I have is only for you." His breath tickled Dayne's ear, and he shivered. "Now let's go or we'll be late."

"Where are we going?"

"I met a woman at work the other day. She had a grease fire in her gas grill, and I put it out for her. She was wonderful and told me she was former Navy. She's also a writer, and she was able to get us into the Carlisle Barracks so we can see the Indian School."

Dayne grinned. "My God." The building was a landmark, but because it was on a military base, getting in to see it could be a problem.

"She's going to meet us there in half an hour, so we need to go." Lawson guided him to the car and drove the fifteen miles through stop-and-go traffic to the entrance to the barracks, where Geri had them park, and she took them in.

He and Lawson had to show identification and explain why they were there. Geri had to accompany them, but eventually they were standing in front of a large, two-story white building with imposing columns in front of both wings of the building.

"This is the main school building," Geri explained, pointing to a central stone structure with a peaked roof. "The dormitories are over there. One was for the boys, and the other for the girls."

"Can we go inside?"

"I got permission," Geri said with a smile. She seemed almost as excited as he did. "Where do you want to go?"

Dayne looked at Lawson. "The boys' dormitory."

If Geri was surprised, she didn't show it. Instead, they walked over, and she opened the door. A long hallway led through the center of the building, with stairs to one end and doors lining the entire route.

"He'd have had an upstairs room, one facing the main building."

"Where are you going?"

"Flying Raven's room. I really want to see it if I can." Dayne climbed the stairs. "It has to be on this side, and it can't be too far down or the view would be obstructed." He opened the door to the first room on the left and stepped inside. There was no furniture and one single window. Dayne could almost imagine bunk beds lining the walls, with dressers for the students to keep their clothes in.

"What are you looking for?" Lawson asked.

"Check the floor. He wrote of a vent. This can't be the room." Dayne left and tried the next one and the one after that. The fourth room was smaller than the others, little more than a closet with a tiny window. Dayne checked the view, and his attention went to the small vent in the wall. "Look. You can see the front of the school, as well as the drive away from it. Is there anything in the vent?" Dayne knew that was a long shot, but Lawson shone a light inside and shook his head.

"Nothing."

Geri had to think they were completely nuts, especially as Dayne began checking the floorboards, walking every inch.

"Look at this. The boards are cut in the same place." Dayne got down on his knees, gently tapped, and tilted the edges until one side lifted a little. He repeated the motion, and Lawson caught the other edge and lifted, exposing a small space under the floor.

Lawson set the boards aside, and Dayne peered into the space. As expected, it was empty. "This has to be where your great-great-uncle's love hid his journals." Dayne grinned, and Lawson shone his light inside. A flash of red caught Dayne's eye, and he pulled out a small red paper heart.

"Oh my God," Lawson whispered as Dayne carefully lifted out the paper, holding it gingerly in his hand.

Dayne stared at the fragile gift of love given over a century earlier. Geri reached into her purse and brought out a small planner, and Dayne put the heart between the pages to protect it. There was nothing else inside, and Lawson put the floorboards back in place. But to Dayne, he might as well have found gold.

"I can't wait to tell Beverly." When he'd returned the journals, he'd told her what he'd found, and she'd read them.

"What is all this about?" Geri asked, and Dayne gave her a brief rundown, talking faster and faster by the second.

"So that heart?"

"Was given to Flying Raven by Soaring Eagle in 1909, and he hid it where he hid the journals. I don't know why he never took it when he took the journals, but it remained in the floor all those years, waiting to be discovered. A token of love." Dayne moved into Lawson's arms. "From two people who helped draw us together."

"Do you want to see more?"

"We can go, and thank you for bringing us." Dayne moved away from Lawson and gave Geri a hug. Then they left the dormitory and went back to the gate, where they thanked Geri again for showing them around. She gave Dayne the heart they'd found, and he placed it between the pages of the car owner's manual to get it home. They waved as Geri left and then they got in the car.

"They did bring us together in a way," Lawson said as he started the engine.

"Yeah. Mostly every time I read the journal, I was reminded how lucky I am. When I needed help most, I found you, the same way Ted found Matthew. And if they could stay together through all they went through and then find their way back together, it gives me hope. They gave me hope."

Lawson turned to him. "The hope came from inside. You always had it, and now good things are happening. I'm taking the captain's exam, and you're brilliant enough to get a scholarship. You're going to make an amazing teacher." Lawson stroked his cheek. "I love you."

Now that was worth anything to hear. Dayne took Lawson's hand and held it in place, not wanting to let go. "I love you too. Now take me home and light a fire."

Lawson didn't have to be told twice.

ANDREW GREY grew up in western Michigan with a father who loved to tell stories and a mother who loved to read them. Since then he has lived all over the country and traveled throughout the world. He has a master's degree from the University of Wisconsin-Milwaukee and now works full-time on his writing. Andrew's hobbies include collecting antiques, gardening, and leaving his dirty dishes anywhere but in the sink (particularly when writing). He considers himself blessed with an accepting family, fantastic friends, and the world's most supportive and loving husband. Andrew currently lives in beautiful historic Carlisle, Pennsylvania.

E-mail: andrewgrey@comcast.net
Website: www.andrewgreybooks.com

REKINDLED FLAME

ANDREW GREY

Rekindled Flame: Book One

Firefighter Morgan has worked hard to build a home for himself after a nomadic childhood. When Morgan is called to a fire, he finds the family out front, but their tenant still inside. He rescues Richard Smalley, who turns out to be an old friend he hasn't seen in years and the one person he regretted leaving behind.

Richard has had a hard life. He served in the military, where he lost the use of his legs, and has been struggling to make his way since coming home. Now that he no longer has a place to live, Morgan takes him in, but when someone attempts to set fire to Morgan's house, they both become suspicious and wonder what's going on.

Years ago Morgan was gutted when he moved away, leaving Richard behind, so he's happy to pick things up where they left off. But now that Richard seems to be the target of an arsonist, he may not be the safest person to be around.

www.dreamspinnerpress.com

CAN'T LIVE
WITHOUT YOU

ANDREW
GREY

Justin Hawthorne worked hard to realize his silver-screen dreams, making his way from small-town Pennsylvania to Hollywood and success. But it hasn't come without sacrifice. When Justin's father kicked him out for being gay, George Miller's family offered to take him in, but circumstances prevented it. Now Justin is back in town and has come face to face with George, the man he left without so much as a good-bye… and the man he's never stopped loving.

Justin's disappearance hit George hard, but he's made a life for himself as a home nurse and finds fulfillment in helping others. When he sees Justin again, George realizes the hole in his heart never mended, and he isn't the only one in need of healing. Justin needs time out of the public eye to find himself again, and George and his mother cannot turn him away. As they stay together in George's home, old feelings are rekindled. Is a second chance possible when everything George cares about is in Pennsylvania and Justin must return to his career in California? First they'll have to deal with the reason for Justin's abrupt departure all those years ago.

www.dreamspinnerpress.com

EYES
ONLY ME
FOR

ANDREW GREY

Eyes of Love: Book One

For years, Clayton Potter's been friends and workout partners with Ronnie. Though Clay is attracted, he's never come on to Ronnie because, let's face it, Ronnie only dates women.

When Clay's father suffers a heart attack, Ronnie, having recently lost his dad, springs into action, driving Clay to the hospital over a hundred miles away. To stay close to Clay's father, the men share a hotel room near the hospital, but after an emotional day, one thing leads to another, and straight-as-an-arrow Ronnie make a proposal that knocks Clay's socks off! Just a little something to take the edge off.

Clay responds in a way he's never considered. After an amazing night together, Clay expects Ronnie to ignore what happened between them and go back to his old life. Ronnie surprises him and seems interested in additional exploration. Though they're friends, Clay suddenly finds it hard to accept the new Ronnie and suspects that Ronnie will return to his old ways. Maybe they both have a thing or two to learn.

www.dreamspinnerpress.com

NOBLE INTENTIONS

ANDREW GREY

Robert Morton is in for the surprise of a lifetime. His mother, a bit of a rebel, raised him away from the rest of the family, and it's not until he's contacted by his lawyer about an inheritance that he learns who he truly is: the new Earl of Hantford. His legacy includes ownership of the historic Ashton Park Estate—which needs repairs Robert cannot afford. He'll simply do what the nobility has done for centuries when in need of money. He'll marry it.

Tech wizard Daniel Fabian is wealthy and successful. In fact, he has almost everything—except a title to make him worthy in the eyes of the old-money snobs he went to prep school with. His high school reunion is looming, and he's determined to attend it as a member of the aristocracy.

That's where Robert comes in.

Daniel has the money, Robert has the name, and both of them know they can help each other out. But their marriage of convenience has the potential to become a real love match—unless a threat to Daniel's business ruins everything.

www.dreamspinnerpress.com

THE
PLAYMAKER
ANDREW GREY

Professional football player Hunter Davis is learning that saying he's gay is very different from actively being in a relationship with another man—especially in the eyes of his teammates and fans. So when Hunter needs a personal assistant to keep him organized, he asks for a woman in order to prevent tongues from wagging.

Montgomery Willis badly needs to find work before he loses everything. There's just one position at the agency where he applies, but the problem is, he's not a woman. And he knows nothing about football. Still, Hunter gives him a chance, but only because Monty's desperate.

Monty soon proves his worth by saving Hunter's bacon on an important promotional shoot, and Hunter realizes he might have someone special working for him—in more ways than one. Monty's feelings come to the surface during an outing in the park when Hunter decides to teach Monty a bit about the game, and pictures surface of them in some questionable positions. Hunter is reminded that knowing he's gay and seeing evidence in the papers are two very different things for the other players, and he might have to choose between two loves: football and Monty.

www.dreamspinnerpress.com

DREAMSPUN DESIRES

POPPY'S SECRET

Andrew Grey

A second chance born of love.

A second chance born of love.

Pat Corrigan and Edgerton "Edge" Winters were ready to start a family—or so Pat thought. At the last minute, Edge got cold feet and fled. Pat didn't bother telling him the conception had already gone through and little Emma was on her way. He didn't want a relationship based on obligation. He'd rather raise his daughter on his own.

Nine years later, Emma and her Poppy are doing fine. Edge isn't. He realizes what he threw away by leaving, and he's back to turn his life around and reclaim his family. It'll take a lot to prove to Pat that he's a new man, and even if Edge succeeds, the secret Pat has hidden for years might shatter their dreams all over again.

www.dreamspinnerpress.com

CPSIA information can be obtained
at www.ICGtesting.com
Printed in the USA
FSOW03n1428250317
32169FS